FRESNO
STORIES

THE NEW DIRECTIONS

Bibelots

KAY BOYLE
THE CRAZY HUNTER

RONALD FIRBANK
CAPRICE

HENRY MILLER
A DEVIL IN PARADISE

EZRA POUND
DIPTYCH ROME-LONDON

WILLIAM SAROYAN
FRESNO STORIES

MURIEL SPARK
THE DRIVER'S SEAT

DYLAN THOMAS
EIGHT STORIES

TENNESSEE WILLIAMS
THE ROMAN SPRING OF MRS. STONE

WILLIAM CARLOS WILLIAMS
ASPHODEL, THAT GREENY FLOWER & OTHER LOVE POEMS

WILLIAM SAROYAN

FRESNO STORIES

A NEW DIRECTIONS

Bibelot

Publisher's note: The eleven stories in this collection were selected from William Saroyan's story collections *Madness in the Family* and *The Man with the Heart in the Highlands*, both available in their entirety from New Directions.

Manufactured in the United States of America
New Directions Books are printed on acid-free paper
Published simultaneously in Canada by Penguin Books Canada Limited
First published as a New Directions Bibelot in 1994

Library of Congress Cataloging-in-Publication Data

Saroyan, William, 1908-1981
    Fresno Stories / William Saroyan.
        p.   cm.
    ISBN 0-8112-1282-3 (acid-free paper)
    I. Title.
  PS3537.A826F74   1994
  813'.52--dc20   94-18355
                                                                CIP

New Directions Books are published for James Laughlin
by New Directions Publishing Corporation,
80 Eighth Avenue, New York 10011

CONTENTS

EARLY STORIES

THE MAN WITH THE HEART
IN THE HIGHLANDS   3

MANY MILES PER HOUR   14

SWEETHEART SWEETHEART
SWEETHEART   23

THE GREAT LEAPFROG CONTEST   31

LATE STORIES

MADNESS IN THE FAMILY   41

FIRE   45

THE INSCRIBED COPY OF THE
KREUTZER SONATA   49

A FRESNO FABLE   60

COWARDS   62

THE LAST WORD WAS LOVE   73

THE DUEL   80

EARLY STORIES

THE MAN WITH THE HEART IN
THE HIGHLANDS

In 1914, when I was not quite six years old, an old man came down San Benito Avenue playing a solo on a bugle and stopped in front of our house. I ran out of the yard and stood at the curb waiting for him to start playing again, but he wouldn't do it. I said, I sure would like to hear you play another tune, and he said, Young man, could you get a glass of water for an old man whose heart is not here, but in the highlands?

What highlands? I said.

The Scotch highlands, said the old man. Could you?

What's your heart doing in the Scotch highlands? I said.

My heart is grieving there, said the old man. Could you bring me a glass of cool water?

Where's your mother? I said.

My mother's in Tulsa, Oklahoma, said the old man, but her heart isn't.

Where *is* her heart? I said.

In the Scotch highlands, said the old man. I am very thirsty, young man.

How come the members of your family are always leaving their hearts in the highlands? I said.

That's the way we are, said the old man. Here today and gone tomorrow.

Here today and gone tomorrow? I said. How do you figure?

Alive one minute and dead the next, said the old man.

Where is your mother's *mother*? I said.

She's up in Vermont, in a little town called White River, but her heart isn't, said the old man.

Is her poor old withered heart in the highlands too? I said.

Right smack in the highlands, said the old man. Son, I'm dying of thirst.

My father came out on the porch and roared like a lion that has just awakened from evil dreams.

Johnny, he roared, get the hell away from that poor old man. Get him a pitcher of water before he falls down and dies. Where in hell are your manners?

Can't a fellow try to find out something from a traveler once in a while? I said.

Get the old gentleman some water, said my father. God damn it, don't stand there like a dummy. Get him a drink before he falls down and dies.

You get him a drink, I said. You ain't doing nothing.

Ain't doing nothing? said my father. Why, Johnny, you know God damn well I'm getting a new poem arranged in my mind.

How do you figure I know? I said. You're just standing there on the porch with your sleeves rolled up. How do you figure I know?

Well, you ought to know, said my father.

Good afternoon, said the old man to my father. Your son has been telling me how clear and cool the climate is in these parts.

4

(Jesus Christ, I said, I never did tell this old man anything about the climate. Where's he getting that stuff from?)

Good afternoon, said my father. Won't you come in for a little rest? We should be honored to have you at our table for a bit of lunch.

Sir, said the old man, I am starving. I shall come right in.

Can you play *Drink to Me Only with Thine Eyes?* I said to the old man. I sure would like to hear you play that song on the bugle. That song is my favorite. I guess I like that song better than any other song in the world.

Son, said the old man, when you get to be my age you'll know songs aren't important, bread is the thing.

Anyway, I said, I sure would like to hear you play that song.

The old man went up on the porch and shook hands with my father.

My name is Jasper MacGregor, he said. I am an actor.

I am mighty glad to make your acquaintance, said my father. Johnny, get Mr. MacGregor a pitcher of water.

I went around to the well and poured some cool water into a pitcher and took it to the old man. He drank the whole pitcherful in one long swig. Then he looked around at the landscape and up at the sky and away up San Benito Avenue where the evening sun was beginning to go down.

I reckon I'm five thousand miles from home, he said. Do you think we could eat a little bread and cheese to keep my body and spirit together?

Johnny, said my father, run down to the grocer's and get a loaf of French bread and a pound of cheese.

Give me the money, I said.

Tell Mr. Kosak to give us credit, said my father. I ain't got a penny, Johnny.

He won't give us credit, I said. Mr. Kosak is tired of giving

5

us credit. He's sore at us. He says we don't work and never pay our bills. We owe him forty cents.

Go on down there and argue it out with him, said my father. You know that's your job.

He won't listen to reason, I said. Mr. Kosak says he doesn't know anything about anything, all he wants is the forty cents.

Go on down there and make him give you a loaf of bread and a pound of cheese, said my father. You can do it, Johnny.

Go on down there, said the old man, and tell Mr. Kosak to give you a loaf of bread and a pound of cheese, son.

Go ahead, Johnny, said my father. You haven't yet failed to leave that store with provender, and you'll be back here in ten minutes with food fit for a king.

I don't know, I said. Mr. Kosak says we are trying to give him the merry run around. He wants to know what kind of work you are doing.

Well, go ahead and tell him, said my father. I have nothing to conceal. I am writing poetry. Tell Mr. Kosak I am writing poetry night and day.

Well, all right, I said, but I don't think he'll be much impressed. He says you never go out like other unemployed men and look for work. He says you're lazy and no good.

You go on down there and tell him he's crazy, Johnny, said my father. You go down there and tell that fellow your father is one of the greatest unknown poets living.

He might not care, I said, but I'll go. I'll do my best. Ain't we got nothing in the house?

Only popcorn, said my father. We been eating popcorn four days in a row now, Johnny. You got to get bread and cheese if you expect me to finish that long poem.

I'll do my best, I said.

Don't take too long, said Mr. MacGregor. I'm five thousand miles from home.

I'll run all the way, I said.

If you find any money on the way, said my father, remember we go fifty-fifty.

All right, I said.

I ran all the way to Mr. Kosak's store, but I didn't find any money on the way, not even a penny.

I went into the store and Mr. Kosak opened his eyes.

Mr. Kosak, I said, if you were in China and didn't have a friend in the world and no money, you'd expect some Christian over there to give you a pound of rice, wouldn't you?

What do you want? said Mr. Kosak.

I just want to talk a little, I said. You'd expect some member of the Aryan race to help you out a little, wouldn't you, Mr. Kosak?

How much money you got? said Mr. Kosak.

It ain't a question of money, Mr. Kosak, I said. I'm talking about being in China and needing the help of the white race.

I don't know nothing about nothing, said Mr. Kosak.

How would you feel in China that way? I said.

I don't know, said Mr. Kosak. What would I be doing in China?

Well, I said, you'd be visiting there, and you'd be hungry, and not a friend in the world. You wouldn't expect a good Christian to turn you away without even a pound of rice, would you, Mr. Kosak?

I guess not, said Mr. Kosak, but you ain't in China, Johnny, and neither is your Pa. You or your Pa's got to go out and work sometime in your lives, so you might as well start now. I ain't going to give you no more groceries on credit because I know you won't pay me.

Mr. Kosak, I said, you misunderstand me: I'm not talking about a few groceries. I'm talking about all them heathen people around you in China, and you hungry and dying.

7

This ain't China, said Mr. Kosak. You got to go out and make your living in this country. Everybody works in America.

Mr. Kosak, I said, suppose it was a loaf of French bread and a pound of cheese you needed to keep you alive in the world, would you hesitate to ask a Christian missionary for these things?

Yes, I would, said Mr. Kosak. I would be ashamed to ask.

Even if you knew you would give him back two loaves of bread and two pounds of cheese? I said. Even then?

Even then, said Mr. Kosak.

Don't be that way, Mr. Kosak, I said. That's defeatist talk, and you know it. Why, the only thing that would happen to you would be death. You would die out there in China, Mr. Kosak.

I wouldn't care if I would, said Mr. Kosak, you and your Pa have got to pay for bread and cheese. Why don't your Pa go out and get a job?

Mr. Kosak, I said, how are you, anyway?

I'm fine, Johnny, said Mr. Kosak. How are you?

Couldn't be better, Mr. Kosak, I said. How are the children?

Fine, said Mr. Kosak. Stepan is beginning to walk now.

That's great, I said. How is Angela?

Angela is beginning to sing, said Mr. Kosak. How is your grandmother?

She's feeling fine, I said. She's beginning to sing too. She says she would rather be an opera star than queen. How's Marta, your wife, Mr. Kosak?

Oh, swell, said Mr. Kosak.

I cannot tell you how glad I am to hear that all is well at your house, I said. I know Stepan is going to be a great man some day.

I hope so, said Mr. Kosak. I am going to send him straight through high school and see that he gets every chance I didn't get. I don't want him to open a grocery store.

I have great faith in Stepan, I said.

What do you want, Johnny? said Mr. Kosak. And how much money you got?

Mr. Kosak, I said, you know I didn't come here to buy anything. You know I enjoy a quiet philosophical chat with you every now and then. Let me have a loaf of French bread and a pound of cheese.

You got to pay cash, Johnny, said Mr. Kosak.

And Esther, I said. How is your beautiful daughter Esther?

Esther is all right, Johnny, said Mr. Kosak, but you got to pay cash. You and your Pa are the worst citizens in this whole county.

I'm glad Esther is all right, Mr. Kosak, I said. Jasper MacGregor is visiting our house. He is a great actor.

I never heard of him, said Mr. Kosak.

And a bottle of beer for Mr. MacGregor, I said.

I can't give you a bottle of beer, said Mr. Kosak.

Certainly you can, I said.

I can't, said Mr. Kosak. I'll let you have one loaf of stale bread, and one pound of cheese, but that's all. What kind of work does your Pa do when he works, Johnny?

My father writes poetry, Mr. Kosak, I said. That's the only work my father does. He is one of the greatest writers of poetry in the world.

When does he get any money? said Mr. Kosak.

He never gets any money, I said. You can't have your cake and eat it.

I don't like that kind of a job, said Mr. Kosak. Why doesn't your Pa work like everybody else, Johnny?

He works harder than everybody else, I said. My father works twice as hard as the average man.

Well, that's fifty-five cents you owe me, Johnny, said Mr. Kosak. I'll let you have some stuff this time, but never again.

Tell Esther I love her, I said.

9

All right, said Mr. Kosak.

Goodbye, Mr. Kosak, I said.

Goodbye, Johnny, said Mr. Kosak.

I ran back to the house with the loaf of French bread and the pound of cheese.

My father and Mr. MacGregor were in the street waiting to see if I would come back with food. They ran half a block toward me and when they saw that it was food, they waved back to the house where my grandmother was waiting. She ran into the house to set the table.

I knew you'd do it, said my father.

So did I, said Mr. MacGregor.

He says we got to pay him fifty-five cents, I said. He says he ain't going to give us no more stuff on credit.

That's his opinion, said my father. What did you talk about, Johnny?

First I talked about being hungry and at death's door in China, I said, and then I inquired about the family.

How is everyone? said my father.

Fine, I said.

So we all went inside and ate the loaf of bread and the pound of cheese, and each of us drank two or three quarts of water, and after every crumb of bread had disappeared, Mr. MacGregor began to look around the kitchen to see if there wasn't something else to eat.

That green can up there, he said. What's in there, Johnny?

Marbles, I said.

That cupboard, he said. Anything edible in there, Johnny?

Crickets, I said.

That big jar in the corner there, Johnny, he said. What's good in there?

I got a gopher snake in that jar, I said.

Well, said Mr. MacGregor, I could go for a bit of boiled gopher snake in a big way, Johnny.

10

You can't have that snake, I said.

Why not, Johnny? said Mr. MacGregor. Why the hell not, son? I hear of fine Borneo natives eating snakes and grasshoppers. You ain't got half a dozen fat grasshoppers around, have you, Johnny?

Only four, I said.

Well, trot them out, Johnny, said Mr. MacGregor, and after we have had our fill, I'll play *Drink to Me Only with Thine Eyes* on the bugle for you. I'm mighty hungry, Johnny.

So am I, I said, but you ain't going to kill that snake.

My father sat at the table with his head in his hands, dreaming. My grandmother paced through the house, singing arias from Puccini. As through the streets I wander, she roared in Italian.

How about a little music? said my father. I think the boy would be delighted.

I sure would, Mr. MacGregor, I said.

All right, Johnny, said Mr. MacGregor.

So he got up and began to blow into the bugle and he blew louder than any man ever blew into a bugle and people for miles around heard him and got excited. Eighteen neighbors gathered in front of our house and applauded when Mr. MacGregor finished the solo. My father led Mr. MacGregor out on the porch and said, Good neighbors and friends, I want you to meet Jasper MacGregor, the greatest Shakespearean actor of our day.

The good neighbors and friends said nothing and Mr. MacGregor said, I remember my first appearance in London in 1867 as if it was yesterday, and he went on with the story of his career. Rufe Apley the carpenter said, How about some more music, Mr. MacGregor? and Mr. MacGregor said, Have you got an egg at your house?

I sure have, said Rufe. I got a dozen eggs at my house.

Would it be convenient for you to go and get one of them

11

dozen eggs? said Mr. MacGregor. When you return I'll play a song that will make your heart leap with joy and grief.

I'm on my way already, said Rufe, and he went home to get an egg.

Mr. MacGregor asked Tom Baker if he had a bit of sausage at his house and Tom said he did, and Mr. MacGregor asked Tom if it would be convenient for Tom to go and get that little bit of sausage and come back with it and when Tom returned Mr. MacGregor would play a song on the bugle that would change the whole history of Tom's life. And Tom went home for the sausage, and Mr. MacGregor asked each of the eighteen good neighbors and friends if he had something small and nice to eat at his home and each man said he did, and each man went to his home to get the small and nice thing to eat, so Mr. MacGregor would play the song he said would be so wonderful to hear, and when all the good neighbors and friends had returned to our house with all the small and nice things to eat, Mr. MacGregor lifted the bugle to his lips and played *My Heart's in the Highlands, My Heart is not Here,* and each of the good neighbors and friends wept and returned to his home, and Mr. MacGregor took all the good things into the kitchen and our family feasted and drank and was merry: an egg, a sausage, a dozen green onions, two kinds of cheese, butter, two kinds of bread, boiled potatoes, fresh tomatoes, a melon, tea, and many other good things to eat, and we ate and our bellies tightened, and Mr. MacGregor said, Sir, if it is all the same to you I should like to dwell in your house for some days to come, and my father said, Sir, my house is your house, and Mr. MacGregor stayed at our house seventeen days and seventeen nights, and on the afternoon of the eighteenth day a man from the Old People's Home came to our house and said, I am looking for Jasper MacGregor, the actor, and my father said, What do you want?

I am from the Old People's Home, said the young man, and I want Mr. MacGregor to come back to our place because we are putting on our annual show in two weeks and need an actor.

Mr. MacGregor got up from the floor where he had been dreaming and went away with the young man, and the following afternoon, when he was very hungry, my father said, Johnny, go down to Mr. Kosak's store and get a little something to eat. I know you can do it, Johnny. Get anything you can.

Mr. Kosak wants fifty-five cents, I said. He won't give us anything more without money.

Go on down there, Johnny, said my father. You know you can get that fine Slovak gentleman to give you a bit of something to eat.

So I went down to Mr. Kosak's store and took up the Chinese problem where I had dropped it, and it was quite a job for me to go away from the store with a box of bird seed and half a can of maple syrup, but I did it, and my father said, Johnny, this sort of fare is going to be pretty dangerous for the old lady, and sure enough in the morning we heard my grandmother singing like a canary, and my father said, How the hell can I write great poetry on bird seed?

Ｗe used to see him going down the highway fifty miles an hour, and my brother Mike used to look kind of sore and jealous.

There he goes, Mike used to say. Where in hell do you think he's going?

Nowhere, I guess, I used to say.

He's in a pretty big hurry for a man who's going nowhere.

I guess he's just turning her loose to see how fast she'll go.

She goes fast enough, Mike used to say. Where the hell can he go from here? Fowler, that's where. That good-for-nothing town.

Or Hanford, I used to say. Or Bakersfield. Don't forget Bakersfield, because it's on the highway. He could make it in three hours.

Two, Mike used to say. He could make it in an hour and three quarters.

Mike was twelve and I was ten, and in those days, 1918, a coupé was a funny-looking affair, an apple-box on four wheels. It wasn't easy to get any kind of a car to go fifty miles an hour, let alone a Ford coupé, but we figured this man had fixed up the motor of his car. We figured he had made a racer out of his little yellow coupé.

We used to see the automobile every day, going down the highway toward Fowler, and an hour or so later we used to see it coming back. On the way down, the car would be traveling like a bat out of hell, rattling and shaking and bouncing, and the man in the car would be smoking a cigarette and smiling to himself, like somebody a little crazy. But on the way back, it would be going no more than ten miles an hour, and the man at the wheel would be calm and sort of slumped down, kind of tired.

He was a fellow you couldn't tell anything about. You couldn't tell how old he was, or what nationality, or anything else. He certainly wasn't more than forty, although he might be less than thirty; and he certainly wasn't Italian, Greek, Armenian, Russian, Chinese, Japanese, German, or any of the other nationalities we knew.

I figure he's an American, Mike used to say. I figure he's a salesman of some kind. He hurries down the highway to some little town and sells something, and comes back, taking it easy.

Maybe, I used to say.

But I didn't think so. I figured he was more likely to be a guy who *liked* to drive down the highway in a big hurry, just for the devil of it.

Those were the years of automobile races: Dario Resta, Jimmie Murphy, Jimmie Chevrolet, and a lot of other boys who finally got killed in racetrack accidents. Those were the days when everybody in America was getting acquainted with the idea of speed. My brother Mike often thought of getting some money somewhere and buying a second-hand car and fixing it up and making it go very fast. Sixty miles an hour maybe. He thought that would be something to do. It was the money, though, that he didn't have.

When I buy my hack, Mike used to say, you're going to see some real speed.

You ain't going to buy no hack, I used to say. What you going to buy a hack with?

I'll get money some way, Mike used to say.

The highway passed in front of our house on Railroad Avenue, just a half-mile south of Rosenberg's Dried Fruit Packing House. Rosenberg's was four brothers who bought figs, dried peaches, apricots, nectarines, and raisins, and put them up in nice cartons and sent them all over the country, and even to foreign countries in Europe. Every summer they hired a lot of people from our part of town, and the women packed the stuff, and the men did harder work, with hand-trucks. Mike went down for a job, but one of the brothers told him to wait another year till he got a little huskier.

That was better than nothing, and Mike couldn't wait to get huskier. He used to look at the pulp-paper magazines for the advertisements of guys like Lionel Strongfort and Earl Liederman, them giants of physical culture, them big guys who could lift a sack of flour over their heads with one arm, and a lot of other things. Mike used to wonder how them big guys got that way, and he used to go down to Cosmos Playground and practice chinning himself on the crossbars, and he used to do a lot of running to develop the muscles of his legs. Mike got to be pretty solid, but not much huskier than he had been. When the hot weather came Mike stopped training. It was too hot to bother.

We started sitting on the steps of our front porch, watching the cars go by. In front of the highway were the railroad tracks, and we could look north and south for miles because it was all level land. We could see a locomotive coming south from town, and we could sit on the steps of our front porch and watch it come closer and closer, and hear it too, and then

16

we could look north and watch it disappear. We did that all one summer during school vacation.

There goes locomotive S. P. 797, Mike used to say.

Yes, sir.

There goes Santa Fe 485321, I used to say. What do you figure is in that box-car, Mike?

Raisins, Mike used to say. Rosenberg's raisins, or figs, or dried peaches, or apricots. Boy, I'll be glad when next summer rolls around, so I can go to work at Rosenberg's and buy me that hack.

Boy, I used to say.

Just thinking of working at Rosenberg's used to do something to Mike. He used to jump up and start shadow-boxing, puffing like a professional fighter, pulling up his tights every once in a while, and grunting.

Boy.

Boy, what he was going to do at Rosenberg's.

It was hell for Mike not to have a job at Rosenberg's, making money, so he could buy his old hack and fix the motor and make it go sixty miles an hour. He used to talk about the old hack all day, sitting on the steps of the porch and watching the cars and trains go by. When the yellow Ford coupé showed up, Mike used to get a little sore, because it was fast. It made him jealous to think of that fellow in the fast car, going down the highway fifty miles an hour.

When I get my hack, Mike used to say, I'll show that guy what real speed is.

We used to walk to town every once in a while. Actually it was at least once every day, but the days were so long every day seemed like a week and it would seem like we hadn't been to town for a week, although we had been there the day before. We used to walk to town, and around town, and then back home again. There was nowhere to go and nothing to do, but we used to get a kick out of walking by the garages and used-car lots on Broadway, especially Mike.

One day we saw the yellow Ford coupé in Ben Mallock's garage on Broadway, and Mike grabbed me by the arm.

There it is, Joe, he said. There's that racer. Let's go in.

We went in and stood by the car. There was no one around, and it was very quiet.

Then the man who owned the car stuck his head out from underneath the car. He looked like the happiest man in the world.

Hello, Mike said.

Howdy, boys, said the man who owned the yellow coupé.

Something wrong? said Mike.

Nothing serious, said the man. Just keeping the old boat in shape.

You don't know us, said Mike. We live in that white house on Railroad Avenue, near Walnut. We see you going down the highway every day.

Oh, yes, said the man. I thought I'd seen you boys somewhere.

My brother Mike, I said, says you're a salesman.

He's wrong, said the man.

I waited for him to tell us *what* he was, if he wasn't a salesman, but he didn't say anything.

I'm going to buy a car myself next year, said Mike. I figure I'll get me a fast Chevrolet.

He did a little shadow-boxing, just thinking about the car, and then he got self-conscious, and the man busted out laughing.

Great idea, he said. Great idea.

He crawled out from under the car and lit a cigarette.

I figure you go about fifty miles an hour, said Mike.

Fifty-two to be exact, said the man. I hope to make sixty one of these days.

18

I could see Mike liked the fellow very much, and I knew I liked him. He was younger than we had imagined. He was probably no more than twenty-five, but he acted no older than a boy of fifteen or sixteen. We thought he was great.

Mike said, What's your name?

Mike could ask a question like that without sounding silly.

Bill, said the man. Bill Wallace. Everybody calls me Speed Wallace.

My name's Mike Flor, said Mike. I'm pleased to meet you. This is my brother Joe.

Mike and the man shook hands. Mike began to shadow-box again.

How would you boys like a little ride? Speed Wallace said.

Oh boy, said Mike.

We jumped into the yellow coupé, and Speed drove out of the garage, down Broadway, and across the railroad tracks in front of Rosenberg's where the highway began. On the highway he opened up to show us a little speed. We passed our house in no time and pretty soon we were tearing down the highway forty miles an hour, then forty-five, then fifty, and pretty soon the speedometer said fifty-one, fifty-two, fifty-three, and the car was rattling like anything.

By the time we were going fifty-six miles an hour we were in Fowler and the man slowed the car down, then stopped. It was very hot.

How about a cold drink? he said.

We got out of the car and walked into a store. Mike drank a bottle of strawberry, and so did I, and then the man said to have another. I said no, but Mike drank another.

The man drank four bottles of strawberry.

Then we got into the car and he drove back very slowly, not more than ten miles an hour, talking all the time about the car, and how fine it was to be able to go down a highway fifty miles an hour.

Do you make money? Mike said.

Not a nickel, Speed said. But one of these days I'm going to build myself a racer and get into the County Fair races, and make some money.

Boy, said Mike.

He let us off at our house, and we talked about the ride for three hours straight.

It was swell. Speed Wallace was a great guy.

In September the County Fair opened. There was a dirt track out there, a mile around. We read advertising cards on fences that said there would be automobile races out there this year.

One day we noticed that the yellow Ford coupé hadn't gone down the highway a whole week.

Mike jumped up all of a sudden when he realized it.

That guy's in the races at the Fair, he said. Come on, let's go.

And we started running down Railroad Avenue.

It was nine in the morning and the races wouldn't begin till around two-thirty, but we ran just the same.

We had to get to the Fair grounds early so we could sneak in. It took us an hour and a half to walk and run to the Fair Grounds, and then it took us two hours more to sneak in. We were caught twice, but finally we got in.

We climbed into the grandstand and everything looked okey-dokey. There were two racing cars on the track, one black, and the other green.

After a while the black one started going around the track. When it got around to where we were sitting we both jumped up because the guy at the wheel was the man who owned the yellow coupé. We felt swell. Boy, he went fast and made a lot of noise. And plenty of dust too, going around the corners.

The races didn't start at two-thirty, they started at three. The grandstands were full of excited people. Seven racing cars

20

got in line. Each was cranked, and the noise they made was very loud and very exciting. Then the race started and Mike started acting like a crazy man, talking to himself, shadow-boxing, and jumping around.

It was the first race, a short one, twenty miles, and Speed Wallace came in fourth.

The next race was forty miles, and Speed Wallace came in second.

The third and last race was seventy-five miles, seventy-five times around the track, and the thirtieth time around Speed Wallace got out in front, just a little way, but out in front just the same: then something went wrong, the inside front wheel of Speed Wallace's racing car busted off and the car turned a furious somersault, away up into the air. Everybody saw Speed Wallace fly out of the car. Everybody saw the car smash him against the wooden fence.

Mike started running down the grandstand, to get closer. I ran after him and I could hear him swearing.

The race didn't stop, but a lot of mechanics got Speed Wallace's wrecked car out of the way, and carried Speed Wallace to an ambulance. While the other cars were going around the track for the seventieth time a man got up and told the people Speed Wallace had been instantly killed.

Holy Christ.

That fellow, Mike said, he got killed. That fellow who used to go down the highway in that yellow Ford coupé, he got killed, Joe. That fellow who gave us a ride to Fowler and bought us drinks.

When it got dark, walking home, Mike started to cry. Just a little. I could tell he was crying from the way his voice sounded. He wasn't really crying.

You remember that swell guy, Joe, he said. He was the one who got killed.

21

We started sitting on the steps of our front porch again, watching the cars go by, but it was sad. We knew the fellow in the yellow Ford coupé wouldn't go down the highway again. Every once in a while Mike would jump up and start shadow-boxing, only it wasn't the way it used to be. He wasn't happy any more, he was sore, and it looked like he was trying to knock hell out of something in the world that caused such a lousy thing like that to happen to a guy like Speed Wallace.

Sweetheart Sweetheart
Sweetheart

O ne thing she *could* do was play the piano and sing. She couldn't cook or anything like that. Anyhow she didn't like to cook because she couldn't make pastry anyway and that's what she liked. She was something like the pastry she was always eating, big and soft and pink, and like a child although she was probably in her late thirties. She claimed she'd been on the stage. *I was an actress three seasons,* is what she told the boy's mother. His mother liked the neighbor but couldn't exactly figure her out. She was married and had no kids, that's what his mother couldn't figure out; and she spent all her time making dresses and putting them on and being very pretty.

Who for? his mother would ask his sister. She would be busy in the kitchen getting food cooked or making bread and in English, which she couldn't talk well but which she liked to talk when she was talking about the neighbor, she said. What for, she's so anxious to be pretty? And then in Italian she'd say, But my, how nice she plays the piano. She's a good neighbor to have.

They'd just moved from one side of town to the other, from Italian town to where the Americans were. This lady was one of them, an American, so his mother guessed that was the way they were, like fancy things to eat, sweet and creamy and soft and pink.

The neighbor used to come over a lot because, she said, it was so refreshing to be among real people.

You know, Mrs. Amendola, she used to say, it's a pleasure to have a neighbor like you. It's so wonderful the way you take care of all your wonderful children without a husband. All your fine growing girls and boys.

Oh, his mother used to laugh, the kids are good. I feed them and take care of them. Headache, toothache, trouble at school, I take care of everything; and his mother roared with laughter. Then his mother looked at the neighbor and said, They're my kids. We fight, we yell, we hit each other, but we like each other. You no got children?

No, the neighbor said. The boy became embarrassed. His mother was so boisterous and abrupt and direct. It was about the third time she'd asked if the neighbor had no children. What she meant, he knew, was, How come you haven't got any? A big woman like you, full of everything to make children?

The neighbor used to come over often when her husband was away. He covered the valley from Bakersfield to Sacramento, selling hardware. Sometimes his wife went with him, but most often not.

She preferred not to because travel was so difficult. And yet whenever she didn't go that meant that she would be in the house alone, and that made her lonely, so she used to visit the Italian family.

One night she came over sobbing and his mother put her arms around the neighbor as if she was one of his mother's kids, and comforted her.

But one thing he noticed that kind of puzzled him; she

wasn't *really* crying. It wasn't honest-to-God crying; it was something else; she wasn't hurt or sorry or in pain or anything; it seemed like she just felt like crying, so she cried, just the same as if she might have felt like buying a dozen cream puffs and eating them. That's the impression he got.

Oh, Mrs. Amendola, she said. I was sitting all alone in the house when all of a sudden I began to remember all the years and then I got scared and started to cry. Oh, I feel so bad, she said and then smiled in a way that seemed awfully lovely to the boy and awfully strange. She looked around at his sister, and then, smiling, she looked at him and he didn't know what to do. She looked a long time. It wasn't a glance. And he knew right away something he didn't understand was going on. She was awfully lovely, big and soft and full of everything, and he felt embarrassed. Her arms were so full.

The little kids were all in bed, so it was only his mother and his sister and him. His mother said, You be all right. You sit with us and talk, you be fine. What's the matter?

I feel so sad, the neighbor said. When I remember all the years gone by, the times when I was a little girl, and then when I was almost grown-up at high school, and then on the stage, I feel so lonely.

Oh, you be all right, his mother said. You like a glass of wine?

His mother didn't wait for her to answer. She got out the bottle and poured two drinks, one for herself and one for the neighbor.

Drink wine, his mother said. Wine is good.

The neighbor sipped the wine.

Oh, it's wonderful, she said. You're a wonderful family, Mrs. Amendola. Won't you come to my house for a visit? I'd like to show you the house.

Oh, sure, his mother said. His mother wanted to see what

her house looked like. So they all went to the house next door and room by room the neighbor showed them the house. It was just like her, like cream puffs. Soft and warm and pink, all except *his* room. He had his own room, bed and everything. There was something fishy somewhere, the boy thought. Americans were different from Italians, that's all he knew. If he slept in one bed and she in another, something was funny somewhere. Her room was like a place in another world. It was so like a woman that he felt ashamed to go in. He stood in the doorway while his mother and sister admired the beautiful room, and then the neighbor noticed him and took his hand. He felt excited and wished he was with her that way alone and in another world. The neighbor laughed and said, But I want *you* to admire my room, too, Tommy. You're such an intelligent and refined boy.

He didn't know for sure, maybe it was his imagination, but when she said he was intelligent and refined it seemed to him she squeezed his hand. He was awfully scared, almost sick. He didn't know about the Americans yet, and he didn't want to do anything wrong. Maybe she *had* squeezed his hand, but maybe it was as if she was just an older person, or a relative. Maybe it was because she was their neighbor, nothing else. He took his hand away as quickly as possible. He didn't speak about the room because he knew anything he'd say would be ridiculous. It was a place he'd like to get in and stay in forever, with her. And that was crazy. She was married. She was old enough to be his mother, although she was a lot younger than his mother. But that was what he wanted.

After they saw the house she cooked chocolate and brought them a cup each. The cups were very delicate and beautiful. There was a plate full of mixed pastry, all kinds of it. She made each of them eat a lot; anyway, for every one she ate, she made them eat one, too, so they each ate four, then there were two left. She laughed and said she could never get enough of pastry, so she was going to take one of the last two, and since Tommy was the man present, he ought to take the other. She said that in a way that more than ever excited the boy. He became confused and deeply mournful about the whole thing. It was something new and out of the world. It was like wanting to get out of the world and never come back. To get into the strange region of warmth and beauty and ease and something else that she seemed to make him feel existed, by her voice and her way of laughing and the way she was, the way her house was, especially the way she looked at him.

He wondered if his mother and sister knew about it. He hoped they didn't. After the chocolate and pastry, his mother asked her to play the piano and sing and she was only too glad to. She played three songs; one for his mother; one for his sister; and then she said, This one for Tommy. She played and sang, *Maytime,* the song that hollers or screams, *Sweetheart sweetheart sweetheart.* The boy was very flattered. He hoped his mother and sister didn't catch on, but that was silly because the first thing his mother said when they got home was, Tommy, I think you got a sweetheart now. And his mother roared with laughter.

She's crazy about you, his sister said.

His sister was three years older than him, seventeen, and she had a fellow. She didn't know yet if she was going to marry him.

She's just nice, the boy said. She was nice to all of us. That's the way she is.

Oh, no, his sister said. She was *nicer* to you than to us. She's falling in love with you, Tommy. Are you falling in love with her?

Aw, shut up, the boy said.

You see, Ma, his sister said. He *is* falling in love with her.

Tell her to cut it out, Ma, the boy said.

You leave my boy alone, his mother told his sister.

And then his mother roared with laughter. It was such a wonderful joke. His mother and his sister laughed until he had to laugh, too. Then all of a sudden their laughter became louder and heartier than ever. It was *too* loud.

Let's not laugh so loud, the boy said. Suppose she hears us? She'll think we're laughing at *her*.

He's in love, Ma, his sister said.

His mother shrugged her shoulders. He knew she was going to come out with one of her comic remarks and he hoped it wouldn't be too embarrassing.

She's a nice girl, his mother said, and his sister started laughing again.

He decided not to think about her any more. He knew if he did his mother and sister would know about it and make fun of him. It wasn't a thing you could make fun of. It was a thing like nothing else, most likely the best thing of all. He didn't want it to be made fun of. He couldn't explain to them but he felt they shouldn't laugh about it.

In the morning her piano-playing wakened him and he began to feel the way he'd felt last night when she'd taken his hand, only now it was worse. He didn't want to get up, or anything. What he wished was that they were together in a room like hers, out of the world, away from everybody, for ever. She sang the song again, four choruses of it, *Sweetheart sweetheart sweetheart*.

His mother made him get up. What's the matter? she said. You'll be late for work. Are you sick?

No, he said. What time is it?

He jumped out of bed and got into his clothes and ate and got on his wheel and raced to the grocery store. He was only two minutes late.

The romance kept up the whole month, all of August. Her

husband came home for two days about the middle of the month. He fooled around in the yard and then went away again.

The boy didn't know what would ever happen. She came over two or three times every week. She appeared in the yard when he was in the yard. She invited the family over to her house two or three times for chocolate and pastry. She woke him up almost every morning singing *Sweetheart sweetheart sweetheart.*

His mother and sister still kidded him about her every once in a while.

One night in September when he got home his sister and mother had a big laugh about him and the neighbor.

Too bad, his mother said. Here, eat your supper. Too bad.

We feel sorry for you, his sister said.

What are you talking about? the boy said.

It's too late now, his mother said.

Too late for *what?* the boy said.

You waited too long, his sister said.

Aw, cut it out, the boy said. What are you talking about?

She's got another sweetheart now, his sister said.

He felt stunned, disgusted, and ill, but tried to go on eating and tried not to show how he felt.

Who? he said.

Your sweetheart, his sister said. You know *who.*

He wasn't sorry. He was angry. Not at his sister and mother; at *her.* She was stupid. He tried to laugh it off.

Well, it's about time, he said.

He comes and gets her in his car, his sister said. It's a Cadillac.

What about her husband? the boy said. He felt foolish.

He don't know! his mother said. Maybe he don't *care.* He's dead, I think.

His mother roared with laughter, and then his sister, too,

29

and then he, too. He was glad Italians laughed, anyway. That made him feel a little better. After supper, though, he was strangely ill all the time. She was a stupid, foolish woman.

Every night for a week his mother and sister told him about the man coming and getting her every afternoon, driving off with her in his Cadillac.

She's got no family, his mother said. She's right. What's the use being pretty for nothing?

He's an awful handsome man, his sister said.

The husband, his mother said, he's dead.

They told him about the neighbor and her lover every night for a week, and then one night she came over to pay another visit. She was lovelier than ever, and not sad any more. Not even make-believe sad.

He was afraid his mother would ask about the man, so he tried to keep her from doing so. He kept looking into his mother's eyes and telling her not to make any mistakes. It would be all right across the tracks, but not in this neighborhood. If *she* wanted to come out with it herself, *she* could tell them. She didn't, though. The boy waited five minutes and then decided she wasn't going to say anything.

He got his cap and said, I'm going to the library, Ma.

All right, his mother said.

He didn't say good night to her. He didn't even look at her. She knew *why*, too.

After that she never played the piano in the mornings, and whenever she *did* play the piano she didn't play the song she'd said was for him.

THE GREAT LEAPFROG
CONTEST

Rosie Mahoney was a tough little Irish kid whose folks, through some miscalculation in directions, or out of an innate spirit of anarchy, had moved into the Russian-Italian-and-Greek neighborhood of my home town, across the Southern Pacific tracks, around G Street.

She wore a turtleneck sweater, usually red. Her father was a bricklayer named Cull and a heavy drinker. Her mother's name was Mary. Mary Mahoney used to go to the Greek Orthodox Catholic Church on Kearny Boulevard every Sunday, because there was no Irish Church to go to anywhere in the neighborhood. The family seemed to be a happy one.

Rosie's three brothers had all grown up and gone to sea. Her two sisters had married. Rosie was the last of the clan. She had entered the world when her father had been close to sixty and her mother in her early fifties. For all that, she was hardly the studious or scholarly type.

Rosie had little use for girls, and as far as possible avoided them. She had less use for boys, but found it undesirable to avoid them. That is to say, she made it a point to take part in everything the boys did. She was always on hand, and always the first to take up any daring or crazy idea. Everybody felt awkward about her continuous presence, but it was no use trying to chase her away, because that meant a fight in which she asked no quarter, and gave none.

If she didn't whip every boy she fought, every fight was at least an honest draw, with a slight edge in Rosie's favor. She didn't fight girl-style, or cry if hurt. She fought the regular style and took advantage of every opening. It was very humiliating to be hurt by Rosie, so after a while any boy who thought of trying to chase her away, decided not to.

It was no use. She just wouldn't go. She didn't seem to like any of the boys especially, but she liked being in on any mischief they might have in mind, and she wanted to play on any teams they organized. She was an excellent baseball player, being as good as anybody else in the neighborhood at any position, and for her age an expert pitcher. She had a wicked wing, too, and could throw a ball in from left field so that when it hit the catcher's mitt it made a nice sound.

She was extraordinarily swift on her feet and played a beautiful game of tin-can hockey.

At pee-wee, she seemed to have the most disgusting luck in the world.

At the game we invented and used to call *Horse* she was as good at *horse* as at *rider,* and she insisted on following the rules of the game. She insisted on being horse when it was her turn to be horse. This always embarrassed her partner, whoever he happened to be, because it didn't seem right for a boy to be getting up on the back of a girl.

She was an excellent football player too.

As a matter of fact, she was just naturally the equal of any boy in the neighborhood, and much the superior of many of them. Especially after she had lived in the neighborhood three years. It took her that long to make everybody understand that she had come to stay and that she was *going* to stay.

She did, too; even after the arrival of a boy named Rex Folger, who was from somewhere in the south of Texas. This boy Rex was a natural-born leader. Two months after his arrival in the neighborhood, it was understood by everyone that if Rex wasn't the leader of the gang, he was very nearly the leader. He had fought and licked every boy in the neighborhood who at one time or another had fancied himself leader. And he had done so without any noticeable ill-feeling, pride, or ambition.

As a matter of fact, no one could possibly have been more good-natured than Rex. Everybody resented him, just the same.

One winter, the whole neighborhood took to playing a game that had become popular on the other side of the tracks, in another slum neighborhood of the town: *Leapfrog*. The idea was for as many boys as cared to participate, to bend down and be leaped over by every other boy in the game, and then himself to get up and begin leaping over all the other boys, and then bend down again until all the boys had leaped over him again, and keep this up until all the other players had become exhausted. This didn't happen, sometimes, until the last two players had traveled a distance of three or four miles, while the other players walked along, watching and making bets.

Rosie, of course, was always in on the game. She was always one of the last to drop out, too. And she was the only person in the neighborhood Rex Folger hadn't fought and beaten.

He felt that that was much too humiliating even to think about. But inasmuch as she seemed to be a member of the gang, he felt that in some way or another he ought to prove his superiority.

One summer day during vacation, an argument between Rex and Rosie developed and Rosie pulled off her turtleneck sweater and challenged him to a fight. Rex took a cigarette from his pocket, lighted it, inhaled, and told Rosie he wasn't in the habit of hitting women—where he came from that amounted to boxing your mother. On the other hand, he said, if Rosie cared to compete with him in any other sport, he would be glad to oblige her. Rex was a very calm and courteous conversationalist. He had poise. It was unconscious, of course, but he had it just the same. He was just naturally a man who couldn't be hurried, flustered, or excited.

So Rex and Rosie fought it out in this game Leapfrog. They got to leaping over one another, quickly, too, until the first thing we knew the whole gang of us was out on the State Highway going south towards Fowler. It was a very hot day. Rosie and Rex were in great shape, and it looked like one was tougher than the other and more stubborn. They talked a good deal, especially Rosie, who insisted that she would have to fall down unconscious before she'd give up to a guy like Rex.

He said he was sorry his opponent was a girl. It grieved him deeply to have to make a girl exert herself to the point of death, but it was just too bad. He had to, so he had to. They leaped and squatted, leaped and squatted, and we got out to Sam Day's vineyard. That was half-way to Fowler. It didn't seem like either Rosie or Rex were ever going to get tired. They hadn't even begun to show signs of growing tired, although each of them was sweating a great deal.

Naturally, we were sure Rex would win the contest. But that was because we hadn't taken into account the fact that he was a simple person, whereas Rosie was crafty and shrewd. Rosie knew how to figure angles. She had discovered how to jump over Rex Folger in a way that weakened him. And after a while, about three miles out of Fowler, we noticed that she was coming down on Rex's *neck,* instead of on his back. Naturally, this was hurting him and making the blood rush to his head. Rosie herself squatted in such a way that it was impossible, almost, for Rex to get anywhere near her neck with his hands.

Before long, we noticed that Rex was weakening. His head was getting closer and closer to the ground. About a half mile out of Fowler, we heard Rex's head bumping the ground every time Rosie leaped over him. They were good loud bumps that we knew were painful, but Rex wasn't complaining. He was too proud to complain.

Rosie, on the other hand, knew she had her man, and she was giving him all she had. She was bumping his head on the ground as solidly as she could, because she knew she didn't have much more fight in her, and if she didn't lay him out cold, in the hot sun, in the next ten minutes or so, she would fall down exhausted herself, and lose the contest.

Suddenly Rosie bumped Rex's head a real powerful one. He got up very dazed and very angry. It was the first time we had ever seen him fuming. By God, the girl was taking advantage of him, if he wasn't mistaken, and he didn't like it. Rosie was squatted in front of him. He came up groggy and paused a moment. Then he gave Rosie a very effective kick that sent her sprawling. Rosie jumped up and smacked Rex in the mouth. The gang jumped in and tried to establish order.

It was agreed that the Leapfrog contest must not change into a fight. Not any more. Not with Fowler only five or ten minutes away. The gang ruled further that Rex had had no right to kick Rosie and that in smacking him in the mouth Rosie had squared the matter, and the contest was to continue.

Rosie was very tired and sore; and so was Rex. They began leaping and squatting again; and again we saw Rosie coming down on Rex's neck so that his head was bumping the ground.

It looked pretty bad for the boy from Texas. We couldn't understand how he could take so much punishment. We all felt that Rex was getting what he had coming to him, but at

35

the same time everybody seemed to feel badly about Rosie, a girl, doing the job instead of one of us. Of course, that was where we were wrong. Nobody but Rosie could have figured out that smart way of humiliating a very powerful and superior boy. It was probably the woman in her, which, less than five years later, came out to such an extent that she became one of the most beautiful girls in town, gave up tomboy activities, and married one of the wealthiest young men in Kings County, a college man named, if memory serves, Wallace Hadington Finlay VI.

Less than a hundred yards from the heart of Fowler, Rosie, with great and admirable artistry, finished the job.

That was where the dirt of the highway siding ended and the paved main street of Fowler began. This street was paved with cement, not asphalt. Asphalt, in that heat, would have been too soft to serve, but cement had exactly the right degree of brittleness. I think Rex, when he squatted over the hard cement, knew the game was up. But he was brave to the end. He squatted over the hard cement and waited for the worst. Behind him, Rosie Mahoney prepared to make the supreme effort. In this next leap, she intended to give her all, which she did.

She came down on Rex Folger's neck like a ton of bricks. His head banged against the hard cement, his body straightened out, and his arms and legs twitched.

He was out like a light.

Six paces in front of him, Rosie Mahoney squatted and waited. Jim Telesco counted twenty, which was the time allowed for each leap. Rex didn't get up during the count.

The contest was over. The winner of the contest was Rosie Mahoney.

Rex didn't get up by himself at all. He just stayed where he was until a half-dozen of us lifted him and carried him to a horse trough, where we splashed water on his face.

Rex was a confused young man all the way back. He was also a deeply humiliated one. He couldn't understand anything about anything. He just looked dazed and speechless. Every now and then we imagined he wanted to talk, and I guess he did, but after we'd all gotten ready to hear what he had to say, he couldn't speak. He made a gesture so tragic that tears came to the eyes of eleven members of the gang.

Rosie Mahoney, on the other hand, talked all the way home. She said everything.

I think it made a better man of Rex. More human. After that he was a gentler sort of soul. It may have been because he couldn't see very well for some time. At any rate, for weeks he seemed to be going around in a dream. His gaze would freeze on some insignificant object far away in the landscape, and half the time it seemed as if he didn't know where he was going, or why. He took little part in the activities of the gang, and the following winter he stayed away altogether. He came to school one day wearing glasses. He looked broken and pathetic.

That winter Rosie Mahoney stopped hanging around with the gang, too. She had a flair for making an exit at the right time.

LATE STORIES

Madness in the Family

Going mad was a specialty of the family. Until a man had gone mad, it was understood that he was still a boy. If he never did, he was not the equal of those who had. Only a few reached the age of thirty unseized, and, over a period of a century, only two or three members of the family went the whole distance unseized. More than a few took the trip several times, after which they were considered wise men, or perhaps even holy men, as if they had made the pilgrimage to Jerusalem, as, in a sense, they had.

With the women it was another matter, although most of them took the trip too; but with the help of the other women in the family, their journeying was fairly well concealed. Women on the trip tended to reject their children, their brothers and sisters, their parents, their parents' parents, and themselves. Their madness was justified and reasonable, which may have made its concealment a relatively simple matter. The demands on women for diplomatic behavior were so severe and so taken for granted by the men that madness was upon the women practically all of the time.

With the men the madness took several traditional forms, including a repudiation of God, or rather of Jesus and Christianity, since nothing but trouble had come of the Fa-

41

ther, the Son, the Holy Ghost, and the Church. Another common form of the madness was a total rejection of the human race, based upon ancient and contemporary evidence that the human race was criminal and contemptible. Oddly, however, this rejection stopped at the threshold of the madman himself, who, during the seizure, whether brief or prolonged, considered himself alone to be the only hope of the human race. His wife was a stranger—some crazy man's daughter. His kids were tricks played on him by shabby genetics. His brothers and sisters were simpletons, his parents sleepwalkers.

Yet another form of the madness was a conviction that all was in vain, all was corrupt, all was useless, all was hopeless.

In Bitlis my father, Manak, was considered wise and worthy because he had made the trip to madness before he was twelve, which was uncommon. During the year of his rage, he went about his life and work pretty much the same as ever, except that people avoided him, because anybody who looked him full in the face saw that he was on his way, and not receptive to small talk. But once the trip was over, there wasn't an easier man to have around. Difficult questions were put to him by the oldest men, which he answered immediately, with unmistakable appropriateness. In the most complicated disputes, he was called upon to pass judgment, and his decisions were instantly accepted by both sides.

When the tribe packed up and came to America, first to New York, and then to California, the family madness continued, but the form changed. Of course, this was to be expected, since America was another kind of place entirely. The whole family hadn't one member buried here. Everybody was on the surface of the country, flat on his feet, selling watermelons, or plowing a row of vines.

We were in Fresno, but we were nowhere, too. How could we really be in a place until death had caught up with one of us, and we had buried him and knew he was there?

This, in fact, was the form the madness took in my Uncle Vorotan, the tailor who worked for Bloom Brothers in their shop on Merced Street.

Each evening when he reached his home, he asked both his wife and his mother, "Has anybody died yet, to heal this fearful loneliness, this aimless walking about, the emptiness and disconnection?" And each evening everybody in every branch of the family was not only still alive but getting stronger and bigger.

Word got around to everybody in the family, including the kids, that Vorotan had gone mad in a new way, compelled by the New World. He wanted somebody to die, and to be buried so that he, as well as the rest of us, might know that a tradition had been established, that a culture must inevitably follow, and that, consequently, we might all be permitted to believe that we were in fact in Fresno, in California, in America, and, in all probability, would stay. Kids, who are supposed to be easy to frighten, rather cherished Vorotan during his madness, even when he looked at one of them and said, "Open your mouth, please," and after looking in, said, "All in order." But some of the older men felt uncomfortable when he looked at them and some of the women, especially those who had married into the family, cried out, "Don't look at me with those eyes. I'm in perfect health, and pregnant!" And later, such a woman might say to her husband, "I really believe he'll kill somebody, so he can go to the funeral, and end his madness, and be at peace with himself again."

If anybody took even slightly ill, everybody in the imme-

43

diate family was cautioned not to let word reach Vorotan, for on several occasions he had gone to the family, to the bed of the one who was ill, and said, "Yes, I believe you will be the one to save us. Do not be afraid, do not hold back, the best Bashmanians are already in that great homeland in the sky, and the rest of us will soon follow." Whereupon the man in bed shouted, "I've got a stupid cold in the head. I'm not going anywhere, but you are, out of this house!"

Vorotan's madness went on and on, because nobody in the family died, even though there were eleven men and women in their eighties.

Early one morning, however, old Varujan, the gunsmith, was found dead in his bed, as if he were only asleep. At last, the Bashmanians had their first dead in the New World. Vorotan was overwhelmed by the good news, donated ten dollars toward the cost of the funeral, made a short talk at the graveside, and was instantly healed of his madness.

"Now, at last, we are here," he said. "We can breathe easier. Varujan, old in years but young in spirit, has saved us all, our first traditionalist in the New World. He is in Ararat, where we shall all go."

Ararat was the Armenian cemetery, which in those days had only a few graves, but is now almost as well populated as Fresno, and with more interesting people, including Vorotan himself.

FIRE

ONE OF THE FEW THINGS all of the Bashmanians are agreed about is fire, which we love, as we do all things in the fire family: the sun, all reds and yellows, California poppies and sunflowers. No wonder the Armenians fought off the Persians when they came with swords to demand that we join them in fire worship. Why should we spoil a good thing by making it official? We had official Jesus, and that was wonder enough.

When a building was on fire in Fresno and the Fire Department came roaring up in its red fire engines, we would already be there, laughing, and rejoicing in the light, heat, color, and music of the fire eating wood to ash.

The greatest fire I ever witnessed was a comparatively insignificant one. The thing that made it great was that it was my house. I had gone with my family in 1919 to Armona—about forty miles southwest of Fresno and three miles from Hanford—where there was good work in the fresh-fruit packing houses, and we shared a house bought for his family by my uncle Gunyaz Bashmanian after he suffered losses in three consecutive business enterprises. A small grocery store on O Street in Fresno went bankrupt because of the lower prices at the big store that suddenly opened next door. Then an orchard of peach and apricot trees in Biola brought forth two crops so meager that the place had to be given back to the bank. And finally this unlucky man bought a jewelry store on Mariposa Street in Fresno, next to D. Yezdan's Clothing Store. One night it was emptied of everything by robbers, who were never apprehended.

"Robbers?" Gunyaz said when he heard of the theft. "Not police?"

Gunyaz put all of his remaining money into the buying of the old house in Armona, so that he and his wife and his two sons could work in the packing houses and perhaps save money again, but his wife took ill, one of his sons broke his arm, and Gunyaz himself sprained his back so badly that even with a brace holding him together he could do no more than stand and walk. When he was almost entirely out of money, with a lot of doctor's bills to pay, Gunyaz took all of his business papers to a lawyer named Jivelikian and asked him to study them carefully. The following day the lawyer said, "I have found all of your papers in order. You paid two thousand dollars cash for the house and its furnishings. I know the house well, as the previous owner asked me to help him sell it three years ago. At best, the furnishings, the house, and the lot on which it stands are all together worth one thousand dollars. However, the fire insurance policy on the house is for six thousand dollars, and has a week to go."

Gunyaz said, "The house is old and rotten. I'm afraid it might catch fire some night when all of us are asleep."

"That is something to avoid at all costs," the lawyer said.

"I can't stand guard every night," Gunyaz said. "I have a bad back and many debts."

"My fee is one dollar," the lawyer said.

Gunyaz paid Jivelikian a silver dollar and went home. As

46

luck would have it, everybody was either at the packing house or at the doctor's, and Gunyaz Bashmanian was home all alone, his head full of sorrow, anger, and fire.

That night, when everybody was home from work or from the doctor's, he said to his wife, "Prepare a feast. We shall enjoy our good health and good fortune in this world, under the fig tree in the back yard."

The feast began a little after ten, by which time I was more sleepy than hungry. Nevertheless, I kept myself awake enough to have a little of everything, and then I began to long for my bed, which I shared with my brother Bakrot Bashmanian, called Buck for short. But Gunyaz said, "No, you must eat now. You are eleven years old; it is not time to go into the house."

He himself went into the house by way of the back door and came out by way of the front door. He returned slowly to the great table under the fig tree, a very solemn and thoughtful man.

Now a nice variety of flashes of light began to come from inside the house, but everybody was having such a good time eating and drinking and talking that I decided that the house was not on fire, and that the flashes of light were only rather large flickerings from three kerosene lamps there. Five minutes later, though, there was a large and crackling light coming from inside the house, and I decided that now the house was on fire, and glad to be. Still, I was better than half asleep and thought I could be dreaming, so I didn't leap to my feet and holler "Fire!"

When I began to feel hot, however, I took Gunyaz by the arm and pointed to the house.

"Wah," he said. "Our house is on fire."

My brother shouted, "I'll go call the Fire Department," and ran off as fast as he could go, barefoot.

"Hurry," Gunyaz shouted after him. "Perhaps we can save something."

Everybody ran to the empty lot next door, and then across the street, where we stood in a religious group, crossing ourselves, as we watched the house being devoured by a big, busy mouth with a ferocious appetite—after which everything fell into the house, and then the fire died. The light went out, the heat ended, the world grew philosophic.

The fire engines came. The happy firemen splattered water on the smoking half-skeleton until all that was left was a lot of wet black cinders where the house had been. A smell of bright living gave way to a smell of dark dying. I wanted to go to sleep. Even so, we were all of us up until long after midnight, and then we found places to sleep on the floors of the houses of various friends who were also in Armona for the summer work.

"How did it start?" somebody asked, and somebody else said, "From the kitchen stove, after cooking."

It was the most beautiful, the most intelligent, the most artful, the sweetest, and the most philosophic fire I ever saw. Even so, I felt especially bad about losing the bed I shared with my brother—the whole thing gone up forever in smoke.

The Inscribed Copy of the Kreutzer Sonata

Gaspar Bashmanian, who understood the enormity and majesty of the human experience, who loved children (the human race of tomorrow, he called them), suddenly became engaged to a girl of seventeen who lived on a muscat vineyard in Reedley with her father and mother, the Apkar Apkarians. These good people threw a great party in honor of the groom-to-be, Gaspar the gentleman, Gaspar the reader of Tolstoy, Gaspar the twenty-seven-year-old philosopher and personal friend of trees.

And everybody was invited.

By horse and buggy, by Ford and Chevrolet, by Dodge and Dort, and by Moon and Kissel Kar, the relatives of both sides began to arrive at the vineyard in Reedley, and I myself, twelve years old, riding with Gaspar in his Overland, arrived there too, just at dusk, at that most somber moment of the day.

And the first thing I heard was the laughter of an unseen girl, a laughter that made me believe everything was worthwhile. Gaspar sat behind the wheel of his open car and listened. The laughter came again, and all I knew was, I loved her, whoever she was, but Gaspar said, "Who is that laughing?"

"Some girl at the party," I said.

"That kind of laughter is no good."

"It *sounds* good."

"It is the laughter of the animal."

We heard the laughter again, and then from around the neat white farmhouse, where the lilac and rose trees stood together like ladies and gentlemen, came running a dark girl dressed all in white, still laughing, herself prettier than her laughter. Chasing the girl were three more girls of her own age, or perhaps a little older, in dresses of green, blue, and red, who were making the sign *shame, shame,* at her, scraping one forefinger upon the other.

"My God," Gaspar said, and I thought he meant how beautiful, how charming, but he went on to say, "how vulgar."

"Who is that girl in the white dress?" I asked God, or anybody.

"I don't know," Gaspar said, "but God help the man who marries her."

Around the house they disappeared, and out of the house came Apkar Apkarian himself, straight to the car, straight to my uncle Gaspar. "Come, my son, come into the house," he said. "What took you so long?"

" 'Slowly to the wedding, slowly to the grave,' " Gaspar said.

"The old sayings are wise sayings," Apkar said, "but there may be sayings we have never heard and shall never hear that may be even wiser. 'Swiftly to the wedding, swiftly away from the killer.' "

"Swiftly away from *what* killer?" Gaspar said.

"Loneliness, my boy," Apkar said. "It is better to be in a lifelong fight with somebody one can see—one's wife, one's children—than to live in the empty peace of the killer who can never be seen. Come along, I'll have her mother bring her to you."

The parlor was a shambles of loud people drinking, singing, talking, and dancing, and after the cheers and the jeers— "Ah, why should you be so lucky, and I so unlucky?"—the girl's father took Gaspar to a far room, followed by her mother, several very old men and women, and four or five boys and girls. In the room was a very large bed, and the father said, "Everybody, sit down, please. And you, woman, go fetch your daughter and present her to Gaspar Bashmanian, her husband-to-be."

I couldn't wait to see who it was that Gaspar was going to marry, and when I saw that it was the laughing girl in the white dress, I felt "What a lucky dog you are," but at the same time I felt "Oh, no, let this one be for me."

As for Gaspar, he tried very hard to conceal his disappointment, and failed. To him, this was the animal girl, and there she stood before him, all composed, deadly serious, and just a little scared, just a little worried about how to *be* because he was a handsome man, perhaps the handsomest she had ever seen, and appropriately severe and demanding. Therefore, she didn't want to make any mistakes that might impel him to notice who and what she really was; but that was precisely what he was noticing—the healthy, bathed, dressed-up daughter of a vineyardist and his illiterate but very wise wife. Should

51

she hold out her hand, small and white and for two weeks rubbed day and night with lotions, or should she bow, or should she smile, or should she just stand there like an exposed fraud and wait?

At last she put out her hand, but when Gaspar didn't go for it instantly, she drew it back, blushing, and then he put out his hand, but now she was bowing, and her hands were clasped behind her back, so that Gaspar had to reach all the way around her to meet her hand on its way back, but as it wasn't on its way back, he withdrew his hand, whereupon the girl straightened up from the bow, brought her hand out again, smiled, her face as red as the petal of a rose, but again Gaspar hesitated, she drew her hand back, and then, slightly pushed by two running small girls who were in her family, she began to lose her balance, reached with both arms to Gaspar for help, he embraced her, but only in order to keep her from falling, she wrapped her arms around him, their heads were almost together, Gaspar forgot his reading and kissed her on the mouth, while the little girls cried out and the little boys whistled, and Apkar said to his wife, "They will have a happy marriage and many children."

Gaspar stopped kissing the girl, but now she kissed him, and the girl's mother said to her father, "A happy marriage and many children, but perhaps not beginning this very minute. Take the young man to the men and let him get drunk, I must talk to my daughter."

At this moment a young man began to sing "Ramona" on a phonograph record.

The mother gently tugged her daughter away from Gaspar, who was taken away by the father saying, "Gaspar, my boy, I have never seen a swifter flowering of love," to which Gaspar, now off cue, replied, "Charmed, I'm sure."

"How about it?" I said. Gaspar glanced at me out of dazed eyes and very swiftly said, "You must read Tolstoy's *The Kreutzer Sonata*."

"Ramona," the phonograph-record singer sang, "I hear the murmurs in the hall."

He heard the *what* in the *where*? But it really didn't matter. We all knew what was going on. Ramona had looked at him, and that was it, he was there at last, and wanted to know of himself, "What took you so long?"

"What did the singer say?" Gaspar said.

" 'Ramona,' " I said.

"I'm sure somebody told me," Gaspar said to the girl's father, "but in the confusing events of the last few minutes, it has slipped my mind—what is your daughter's *name*?"

"Araxie. But everybody calls her Roxie. When is the wedding to be, my boy? Next Saturday?"

"What's he saying *now*—that singer?" Gaspar said to me.

" 'Ramona, Ramona.' What do you care what he's saying? What are *you* saying?"

But now we were back in the room where the party was going on. Gaspar was handed a small tumbler full of the white firewater of our people, made by Apkar himself out of his own muscat raisins, with his own still, a hundred or more gallons a year, enough for everybody, raki, unlicensed, tax-free, one hundred proof, and other proof as well, proof of being there, for instance, thick in the fight, nobody will ever see youth again, except in the faces of his own kids, "Drink, Gaspar, everybody drink to Gaspar." But a man of the opposition called back, "Why should we drink to him, cleaned and pressed? We drink to our girl, Roxie Apkarian, the dark Rose of Gultik." Was somebody being insulted *already*, long before the wedding?

"Be careful, please," somebody unseen on our side said. "We drink to our boy, Gaspar, also of Gultik. There are many Roses of Gultik for Gaspar to pluck, remember that, friends, and be careful."

"By turns let us drink to each other," Apkar roared. "There is plenty to drink. By turns to each, and soon enough we'll all be drunk. We are all from Gultik, in our beloved Hayastan. Everybody drink to Gaspar."

"Wrong, entirely wrong, the girl comes first. Everybody drink to Roxie."

"Are we being insulted?"

"Take it as you like, the girl comes first. Since when are rules to be broken?"

"Careful, please."

All of the men and the boys who weren't already standing got to their feet, all fists that weren't clenched became clenched, all except Gaspar's. He looked around at the men of the opposition, and then at the men on his side, and then, again off cue, said, "It is indeed an honor."

"Bet your life it is," somebody growled. "Where do you come from to take the hand of our beautiful girl, Roxie?"

"2832 Ventura Avenue," Gaspar said.

"Not far enough away. Who cares about your broken-down house at 2832 Ventura Avenue? Is that a suitable place to take our Roxie?"

The sides, with lifted glasses in one hand, fists raised slightly, began to move toward each other, and then Gaspar

54

said, "I deem it a privilege and an honor to drink to Miss Araxie Apkarian."

Whereupon he gulped down the contents of his glass, impelling everybody else to do the same, each drinker cheering or breaking into song.

Thus, the fight, the *inevitable* fight, was postponed—but for how long? That was the question.

Somebody put needle to disk, the singer took off about Ramona again, and although the phonograph was in the corner of the room, and loud, everybody who had anything to say was heard by everybody else, and almost immediately the fight began to shape up again. One of the Roxie boys said to one of the Gaspar boys, "And just who do you think you are?"

"Trigus Trolley."

"Who?"

"You heard me."

"There's no such name."

"There is *now*."

"You're one of the Bashmanians, that's who you are."

"You asked me who I am and I told you. If you want to fight, fight, don't argue."

"The Apkarians don't fight in the parlor, the way the Bashmanians do."

"If they don't fight in the parlor, they'd better not ask for a fight in the parlor."

"Just wait until the fight starts, I'll get you."

"You'll get me the way the cat gets the dog that chases her up the tree."

"Who do you think you are to call me a cat?"

"Fight, or go back where you came from."

Roxie's mother went to the boys and said, "Don't fight,

we are all in the same burning house." Another proverb, or saying of the people of Gultik.

And then she went around among all of the men and said something to each of them, so that all we did for the next couple of hours was eat and drink and sing and dance, and then suddenly Gaspar was hit in the nose. He in turn instantly knocked down the man who had hit him, and I ran across the room to a boy who was ready and waiting, who knocked me down—a terrible surprise and insult.

I leaped to my feet, but already the whole fight was over. Apologies were made, admiration was expressed by each side for the other, wounds were treated, drinks were poured and handed around, broken glass was picked up, the needle was put to disk, and the singer began to sing "Ramona" again.

On our way home, zigzagging in the Overland down the empty country road—going in the wrong direction—Gaspar said, "*The Kreutzer Sonata.*"

"What about it?"

"I must read it again as soon as possible—tonight, perhaps."

"Why?"

"It is a story by Tolstoy about marriage."

"What happens in the story?"

"Everything, and all wrong," Gaspar groaned.

The wedding had been scheduled for four weeks later, another Saturday night, but the Saturday before the wedding, Gaspar took Roxie to a movie in Reedley, and then to an ice-cream parlor, and the next day he said, "My God."

"She's the most beautiful girl in the world," I said.

"Beautiful, yes," Gaspar said. "Just like in *The Kreutzer Sonata*, but beauty, *real* beauty, must come from inside, from the heart, from the mind, from the spirit."

"*Her* beauty comes from all over."

"I wish it did, but it doesn't."

"Something happened," I said. "What happened?"

"She lives on a material plane," Gaspar said. "She thinks only of material things. She wants to know what kind of a house are we going to have. How are we going to save money to get a *better* house? What kind of car? What kind of furniture? What kind of clothes? If that's the way she is *now*, how is she going to be after she becomes my wife?"

"She'll be just fine," I said. "You're one of the luckiest men in the world."

"If only *she* lived on a spiritual plane, too," Gaspar said.

"*Teach* her to live on a spiritual plane. That's your territory."

"I am trying," Gaspar said. "Two weeks ago I gave her a copy of *The Kreutzer Sonata*, inscribed from me to her."

"Did she read it?"

"She *says* she read it, but it doesn't seem to have had any effect on her at all."

"Maybe it's not the right kind of book for her."

"She asked me to buy her a wristwatch. *Asked* me."

"Buy her one."

"I must think about this. Very carefully."

The wedding was postponed three times, and then Roxie Apkarian became engaged to a dentist who had just come out to California from Boston, and Gaspar said, "There, you see. It wasn't love. She never loved me."

He got into his Overland.

"Where to?" I said, jumping in.

"I'm going out there to kill the dentist."

He went out there.

Roxie cried and ran away from a face-to-face confrontation with him and refused to come out of her room, and her father said, "Gaspar, my boy, she does not love the dentist, she loves you."

Two weeks later her engagement to the dentist was broken, the engagement to Gaspar was on again, the wedding was scheduled for a month later, and this time it took place on schedule.

The men of the opposition at the wedding party jeered, saying, "Gaspar, oh, Gaspar, how about tonight?" And Roxie's women cursed their men and said, "How about right now if Roxie feels like it? Right here in the parlor?"

"A man's world, to be sure," one of the prettier women said, "and a rather spiritual sort of world at that, too, but just let Roxie tug at the top of her silk stocking and whose world would it be then?"

As it is in this world and life, for the people of Gultik as well as most others, in almost no time at all they were the parents of four boys and three girls, it had been a rough fight all the way, Roxie herself broke the "Ramona" phonograph record. And into every fight came the inscribed copy of *The Kreutzer Sonata*, first as a guide to silly sorrow, and then as a weapon thrown by Roxie Apkarian straight at the head of the philosophical, spiritual inscriber, Gaspar Bashmanian, "May we always live on a high Tolstoyan plateau of deep socialistic truth and humanitarian beauty."

In short, don't count on being terribly spiritual unless you are also always slightly sick.

A proverb overlooked by Gultik, but seized upon eagerly by Fresno.

A FRESNO FABLE

KEROPE ANTOYAN, the grocer, ran into Aram Bashmanian, the lawyer, in the street one day and said, "Aram, you are the very man I have been looking for. It is a miracle that I find you this way at this time, because there is only one man in this world I want to talk to, and you are that man, Aram."

"Very well, Kerope," the lawyer said. "Here I am."

"This morning," the grocer said, "when I got up I said to myself, 'If there is anybody in this whole world I can trust, it is Aram,' and here you are before my eyes—my salvation, the restorer of peace to my soul. If I had hoped to see an angel in the street, I would not have been half so pleased as I am to see you, Aram."

"Well, of course I can always be found in my office," Aram said, "but I'm glad we have met in the street. What is it, Kerope?"

"Aram, we are from Biltis. We understand all too well that before one speaks one thinks. Before the cat tastes the fish, his whiskers must feel the head. A prudent man does not open an umbrella for one drop of rain. Caution with strangers, care with friends, trust in one's very own—as you are my very own, Aram. I thank God for bringing you to me at this moment of crisis."

"What is it, Kerope?"

"Aram, every eye has a brow, every lip a mustache, the foot wants its shoe, the hand its glove, what is a tailor without his needle, even a lost dog remembers having had a bone, until a candle is lighted a prayer for a friend cannot be said, one man's ruin is another man's reward."

"Yes, of course, but what is the crisis, Kerope?"

"A good song in the mouth of a bad singer is more painful to the ear than a small man's sneeze," the grocer said.

"Kerope," the lawyer said. "How can I help you?"

"You are like a brother to me, Aram—a younger brother whose wisdom is far greater than my own, far greater than any man's."

"Well, thank you, Kerope," Aram said, "but *please* tell me what's the matter, so I can try to help you."

In the end, though, Kerope refused to tell Aram his problem.

Moral: If you're really smart, you won't trust even an angel.

COWARDS

COWARDS ARE THE NICEST PEOPLE, the most interesting, the gentlest, the most refined, the least likely to commit crimes. They wouldn't think of robbing a bank. They have no wish to assassinate a President. If a ditchdigger calls him a bastard for accidentally kicking dirt into his eyes, a coward doesn't feel his honor has been sullied and he must therefore fight the ditchdigger and take an awful beating. He says, "I'm sorry, I really didn't mean to do that," and goes about his business.

Cowards are decent. They are thoughtful.

When the Selective Service Act reached into Armenian Town in Fresno in 1917, the eligible sons of the various families making their homes there presented themselves to the draft board in the hall of Emerson School and were soon in training camp at Camp Curry in Yosemite National Park. The government wanted them, who were they to argue with the government?

At this time, however, a man of twenty-four named Kristofor Agbadashian, who lived with his mother and three unmarried sisters in the house at number 123 M Street, who for three years had been employed at Cooper's Department Store in the menswear department, disappeared.

Suddenly it was noticed that he did not leave his house

precisely at 8:15 every morning and walk to work, easily the best-dressed man in the whole neighborhood, right down to the pearl stickpin in his tie and the red rosebud in his lapel. Well, of course, a lot of young men in the neighborhood had been drafted and had disappeared, so there was no reason for anybody to wonder about the actual whereabouts of Kristofor. Inquiries about him at Cooper's were answered by the remark that he was away, which, of course, was true.

As for his mother, whenever one of the mothers of the neighborhood who had had one or two sons drafted discreetly, cautiously, and even sympathetically asked about the where-abouts and well-being of Kristofor, saying perhaps, "Ahkh, my dear Aylizabet, I miss seeing handsome Kristofor on his way to work every morning, has the poor boy been drawn into the war by the government, as my Simon and Vask have been?" Kristofor's mother said, "Yes, Kristofor has been taken also. God protect him, and your sons as well."

And of course there was no reason for anybody to disbelieve this reply, or to look into the matter further. However, when official-looking Fords and Chevrolets stopped in front of the neat white little house at 123 M Street, and important-looking Americans stepped out of these automobiles and went up to the front door, and then on into the house, everybody in the neighborhood began to wonder what was going on. Was it possible that Kristofor had already lost his life, and the important-looking Americans, surely employed by the government, were calling on the boy's mother and sisters to break the word gently, and to pay homage to Kristofor for being the first in Armenian Town to give his life for the government? But when a month later *three* cars stopped in front of the house and more important-looking people than ever stepped out of the cars, including a man wearing a sheriff's badge and a revolver in holster, the people of the neighborhood began to suspect that something might be not quite right.

Packing figs at Guggenheim's, the mother Aylizabet one day said to her best friend, Arshaluce Ganjakian, "Please try to understand my nervousness. I can't sleep, I can't rest, for anxiety about my son. We believed he had been taken into the Army, the same as all of our other boys, but they tell us no, he isn't in the Army, so then, my dear Arshaluce, where is he? It would be a thousand times better if he were in the Army, and sent me a letter once a month. Six months now, and not one word. I can only pray that nothing terrible has happened to him."

"Ah, he's a good boy," the friend said. "God will look after him, although I hope he hasn't gone somewhere and lost himself in a life of sin. In a big city like San Francisco perhaps, or Chicago, or even New York. I will light a candle for him at church this Sunday and say a prayer, for he is a good boy." And then, after working swiftly in silence for half an hour or more, to earn perhaps as much as two dollars for a ten-hour day, the friend said, "Or, what's worse even than a life of sin somewhere, I pray to God he hasn't gone to a river and drowned himself, as other young men have done, because they do not believe in war and refuse to be soldiers. Only night before last my youngest, Yedvard, read about such a boy in *The Evening Herald*."

"Drowned himself?" Aylizabet said.

"In Kings River," the friend said. "Wrote his note, took off his clothes, and drowned himself."

"Poor boy, whoever he was."

"A German boy. There are many of them in Kingsburg."

"Poor dear German boy, how can the government ask him to kill his own brothers?"

"Nobody can help *him*," the friend said. "He's gone. The police suspected a trick, dragged the river, found his body, and so his people buried him, but nobody went to the funeral except his own father and mother and brothers and sisters. It was all in the paper, which said friends of the family were afraid to go to the funeral, since they are all Germans."

"The poor father, the poor mother, the poor little brothers and sisters," Aylizabet said. "I love them all, whoever they are."

"Germans," Arshaluce said. "Enemies. All of a sudden they are enemies, but after the war will they still be enemies? The boy will still be drowned. Even a life of sin in a big city is better than to be drowned, because after the war the sinner will still be alive, at any rate. There is always such a thing as redemption. He can start all over again. He can speak to the Holy Father at the Holy Church and be born again. He can take a nice Armenian girl for his wife and start a family of his own. A life of sin, any life at all, is better than to be drowned, because the war will end, every war ends, and he will still be only a young man. I will light a candle and say a prayer for Kristofor. Do not be nervous about your son, Aylizabet, there is a God in Heaven."

And so the new word in the neighborhood about Kristofor was, "He is gone, he has disappeared, he has written his mother no letter in six months, he may be living a life of sin in San Francisco, or he may have drowned himself, remember him in your prayers."

And there the matter stood for many months.

Haigus Baboyan mailed postcards from Paris of the Eiffel Tower, the Arc de Triomphe, and the Tuileries to the nine members of the Sunday School class he had taught at the First Armenian Presbyterian Church, saying uplifting things like, "The streets of Paris are full of men born crippled because of syphilis in their fathers." And so on.

Gissag Jamanakian was killed at Verdun, Vaharam Vaharamian at Chateau-Thierry, and the Kasabian twins, Krikor and Karekin, at Belleau Wood. All under twenty-five years of age, all brought to Fresno from Armenia when they were still babes in arms or small boys. But there were many others, too—killed in action in France, in Flanders Field, in Normandy, or somewhere else. A number of unlucky fellows died at Camp Curry of influenza, almost as if they hadn't been in the war at all. Two or three went over the hill from that camp to San Francisco, but after a week or two returned, were given medical examinations, and then were only mildly punished. A half-dozen boys of the neighborhood were gassed, but survived. And Hovsep Lucinian, hit by shrapnel and left for dead in an area under bombardment called no-man's-land, made his peace with himself and considered himself as good as dead when somebody came crawling and dragged him to safety. This turned out to be the one man in his company Hovsep hadn't liked, had in fact considered an enemy—an Assyrian boy from

Turlock named Joe Assouri. They became friends for life, although they had frequent fallings-out, whereupon Joe would shout, "I was a damned fool to risk my life to save yours." And Hovsep would shout back, "I am only waiting for the day when I shall be able to save your life. After that, forget it." These outbursts were at poker games, when both men had large families of kids by American girls. Kids who spoke neither Armenian nor Assyrian but kept their names and looked for all the world precisely as they should—altogether Assyrian and Armenian, but with just a little something unaccountable added.

In Guggenheim's, early in October of 1918, Kristofor's mother Aylizabet said to her best friend, Arshaluce Ganjakian, "Is it true that the war will soon end?"

"Yes," Arshaluce said, "Yedvard reads about it in *The Evening Herald* every night. Soon now our boys will all come home. I shall see my Mihran soon, and you will see your Kristofor, I'm sure, wherever he is. Have you still had no word?"

"None," Aylizabet said. "Almost two full years, not one word."

But for longer than a year the whole neighborhood *had* had word about Kristofor, which they both believed and disbelieved. It came about because of something said by Ash Bashmanian, who, after selling papers every evening, went to the Liberty Theater because admission for him was only a copy of the paper handed to the ticket-taker, and did not leave until after the last show, which for Fresno was rather late, a little before midnight. When Ash got home and sat down to his supper he told his father, "I saw Kristofor tonight."

After a few minutes his father said, "I wasn't listening.

67

I'm worried about you at the movies every night. What did you say?"

"Kristofor," Ash said. "I saw him."

"Kristofor Agbadashian?"

"Yes. The Cooper's menswear man."

"You imagined it," the father said. "From seeing so many movies."

"No, I saw him."

"He's been gone almost two whole years. How could you see him?"

"He came back, I guess," Ash said.

"From where?" the father said. "Was he in uniform?"

"No, he was wearing the same clothes he always wears."

"Where'd he go?"

"Home."

"What home?"

"On M Street. I saw him go into his house, and I came on home."

"Keep this to yourself, please," the father said.

"Why?"

"Just keep it to yourself. You can't see straight from seeing movies, and Kristofor is wanted by the government. Let's forget all about it. You didn't see anything. I'll give you a dollar."

"I don't want a dollar," Ash said. "I sell papers every day to bring home money, to help out. I won't tell anybody, but I *did* see him."

Somebody else must have seen him, too, because it was soon all over the neighborhood that Kristofor Agbadashian was home. He had either run away and come back, or he had been hiding in the house at 123 M Street all the time, until finally it had become too much for him and he had taken to going out to walk late at night.

"Where's he been?" the joke went.

"Under the bed," came the answer.

And so, of course, the word of the neighborhood had reached Kristofor's mother's best friend, Arshaluce Ganjakian, if, in fact, it had not also reached Kristofor's mother herself.

A few days after their talk about the probability that the war would soon end, Aylizabet Agbadashian said to Arshaluce Ganjakian, "Arshaluce, my dear friend, I must tell you something on our way home from work tonight, or I'm afraid I shall die." On their way home, when she was sure no one else would overhear them, she said, "Kristofor did not go anywhere. He has been home all this time. It is my fault. I told him I would die if he went away. His father died when he was still a small boy. I could not bear to lose the only man remaining in my family. But now what shall I do? What will happen to him when the war ends and everybody comes home? It is all my fault, not his, I swear it. Help me. I know I can trust you not to tell anybody, but please help me, and someday I will help you. What shall I do? What shall we do?"

On November 11, 1918, the war ended. And that was that, except for the drowned boy in Kingsburg, the dead of the neighborhood in France, the dead from influenza at Camp Curry, and the disgraced Kristofor Under the Bed, as he came to be called by everybody. But nobody looked down at him, and nobody looked down at his mother. Only Kristofor and his mother knew what they had done and why they had done it. Nobody else could even guess. Whatever it had been, *however* it had been, it was something between themselves and God alone, not the government, which of course had much, much more between itself and God alone.

For weeks and months, as the boys of the neighborhood came home and got back into their proper clothes, there was happy confusion in Armenian Town, with only an occasional outbreak of sorrow, and almost always on the part of the strongest men, such as Shulavary Bashmanian, who, when he was asked for whom he was crying, since he had had no son in the war, said, "For Kristofor. Crucified for his bravery. Coward he was, no doubt, but how much more brave a man must be to be a coward. It is easy to be a soldier of the government with all of your comrades. But it is very hard to be yourself, all alone under the bed in your mother's house. I am crying for the bravery of Kristofor. The war is over. Whoever won, won *without* Kristofor. May God forgive the winners and the loser alike, they each have their dead. May God protect Kristofor Under the Bed, wherever he may be or wherever he may go."

As a matter of fact, several weeks before the signing of the Armistice, he went to Sacramento and under the name of Charles Abbott took a job in the menswear department of Roos Bros., who soon invited him to take a better job at more money at the store in San Francisco, where he stayed for three years, at which time he opened his own store on Post Street.

It was there six years later that the government caught up with him. He was married to a Scotch-Irish girl from Boston, a graduate of Smith, and they had had three sons and a daughter. Two of his sisters had married, one had died, and his mother lived alone in the house at 123 M Street, now and then visited by her daughters and their husbands and kids.

The man from the government, who was in his late sixties, by name Battaglia, said, "What we want to do most of all is close out these cases and forget them. You are Kristofor Agbadashian, then?"

"Yes," Kristofor said, "although, as you know, I have been using another name—Charles Abbott—for about ten years. I had always had in mind making the change in any case, as my true name is difficult for the American tongue, and my maternal grandfather's name was Ahpet, which is very nearly the same as Abbott."

"Yes, that's sensible," Battaglia said. "A case of amnesia, would you say?"

"No," Kristofor said. "It wasn't amnesia. I hid, in my own house, because I didn't want to go. I knew what I was doing. My mother and my sisters begged me every day to give myself up and go into the Army, but I refused. I haven't forgotten any of it. There has been no amnesia. And my life has proven itself too well for me to feel embarrassed about, or ashamed of, it. In my hometown I'm still remembered by a handful of very decent people as Kristofor Under the Bed. I am beginning to tell my kids about it, too. So far they think it's very funny."

"I understand," Battaglia said. "Under this line, Cause of Failure to Present Self, I have been putting down Amnesia, in case anybody takes it into his head to examine these forms, which isn't very likely. What do you suggest I put on your form?"

"Coward," Kristofor said.

"That would be as inaccurate as Amnesia," Battaglia said. He wrote in the space, and said, "Father. That'll do it, I'm sure. The case is closed." He left the shop, as if he had gone in to buy something and hadn't seen anything that suited him.

Cowards are nice, they're interesting, they're gentle, they wouldn't think of shooting down people in a parade from a tower. They want to live, so they can see their kids. They're very brave.

A LONG TIME AGO when I was eleven my mother and my father had a prolonged quarrel.

The quarrel picked up the minute my father got home from work at Graff's, where he was a forty-seven-year-old assistant—to everybody. Graff's sold everything from food to ready-made clothing, animal traps, and farm implements. My father had taken the job only for the daily wage of three dollars, which he received in coin at the end of every twelve-hour day. He didn't mind the nature of the work, even though his profession was teaching, and he didn't care that it might end at any moment, without notice.

He'd already had the job six months, from late summer to early spring, when the quarrel began to get on my brother's nerves. I didn't even begin to notice the quarrel until Ralph pointed it out to me. I admired him so much that I joined him in finding fault with my mother and father.

First, though, I'd better describe the quarrel, if that's possible.

To begin with, there was my mother running the house, and there was my father working at Graff's. There was my brother, Ralph, at the top of his class at high school. There I was near the bottom of my class at junior high. And there was our nine-year-old sister, Rose, just enjoying life without any fuss.

All I can say about my mother is that she was a woman—to me a very beautiful one. She had a way of moving very quickly from a singing-and-laughing gladness to a silent-and-dark discontent that bothered my father. I remember hearing him say to her again and again, "Ann, what *is* it?"

Alas, the question was always useless, making my mother cry and my father leave the house.

During the long quarrel my father seemed hopelessly perplexed and outwitted by something unexpected and unwelcome, which he was determined nevertheless to control and banish.

My brother, Ralph, graduated from high school and took a summertime job in a vineyard. He rode eleven miles to the vineyard on his bicycle every morning soon after daybreak and back again a little before dark every evening. His wages were twenty-five cents an hour, and he put in at least ten hours a day. Early in September he had saved a little more than a hundred dollars.

Early one morning he woke me up.

"I want to say good-bye now," he said. "I'm going to San Francisco."

"What for?"

"I can't stay here any more."

Except for the tears in his eyes, I believe I would have said, "Well, good luck, Ralph," but the tears made that impossible. He was as big as my father. The suit he was wearing was my father's, which my mother had altered for him. What were the tears for? Would I have them in my own eyes in a moment, too, after all the years of imitating him to never have

74

them, and having succeeded except for the two or three times I had let them go when I had been alone, and nobody knew? And if the tears came into my eyes, too, what would they be for? Everything I knew I'd learned from my brother, not from school, and everything he knew he'd learned from my father. So now what did we know? What did my father know? What did my brother? What did I?

I got out of bed and jumped into my clothes and went outside to the backyard. Under the old sycamore tree was the almost completed raft my brother and I had been making in our spare time, to launch one day soon on Kings River.

"I'll finish it alone," I thought. "I'll float down Kings River alone."

My brother came out of the house quietly, holding an old straw suitcase.

"I'll finish the raft," I said. I believed my brother would say something in the same casual tone of voice, and then turn and walk away, and that would be that.

Instead, though, he set the suitcase down and came to the raft. He stepped onto it and sat down, as if we'd just launched the raft and were sailing down Kings River. He put his hand over the side, as if into the cold water of Kings River, and he looked around, as if the raft were passing between vineyards and orchards. After a moment he got up, stepped out of the raft, and picked up the suitcase. There were no tears in his eyes now, but he just couldn't say goodbye. For a moment I thought he was going to give up the idea of leaving home and go back to bed.

Instead, he said, "I'll never go into that house again."

"Do you hate them? Is that why?"

"No," he said, but now he began to cry, as if he were eight or nine years old, not almost seventeen.

I picked up the raft, tipped it over, and jumped on it until some of the boards we had so carefully nailed together broke. Then I began to run. I didn't turn around to look at him again.

I ran and walked all the way to where we had planned to launch the raft, about six miles. I sat on the riverbank and tried to think.

It didn't do any good, though. I just didn't understand, that's all.

When I got home it was after eleven in the morning, I was very hungry, and I wanted to sit down and eat. My father was at his job at Graff's. My sister was out of the house, and my mother didn't seem to want to look at me. She put food on the table—more than usual, so I was pretty sure she knew something, or at any rate suspected.

At last she said, "Who smashed the raft?"

"I did."

"Why?"

"I got mad at my brother."

"Why?"

"I just got mad."

"Eat your food."

She went into the living room, and I ate my food. When I went into the living room she was working at the sewing machine with another of my father's suits.

"This one's for you," she said.

"When can I wear it?"

"Next Sunday. It's one of your father's oldest, when he was slimmer. It'll be a good fit. Do you like it?"

"Yes."

She put the work aside and tried to smile, and then *did*, a little.

"She doesn't know what's happened," I thought. And then I thought, "Maybe she *does*, and this is the way she is."

"Your brother's bike is in the garage," she said. "Where's *he*?"

"On his way to San Francisco."

"Where have *you* been?"

"I took a walk."

"A *long* walk?"

"Yes."

"Why?"

"I wanted to be alone."

My mother waited a moment and then she said, "Why is your brother on his way to San Francisco?"

"Because—" But I just couldn't tell her.

"It's all right," she said. "Tell me."

"Because you and Pop fight so much."

"*Fight?*"

"Yes."

"*Do we?*" my mother said.

"I don't know. Are you going to make him come home? Is Pop going to go and get him?"

"No."

"Does he *know*?"

"Yes. He told me."

"When?"

"Right after you ran off, and your brother began to walk to the depot. Your father saw the whole thing."

"Didn't he want to stop him?"

"No. Now, go out and repair the raft."

I worked hard every day and finished the raft in two weeks. One evening my father helped me get it onto a truck he'd hired. We drove to Kings River, launched it, and sailed down the river about twelve miles. My father brought a letter out of his pocket and read it out loud. It was addressed to Dear Mother and Father. All it said was that Ralph had found a job that he liked, and was going to go to college when the fall semester began, and was well and happy. The last word of the letter was love.

My father handed me the letter and I read the word for myself.

That Christmas my father sent me to San Francisco to spend a few days with my brother. It was a great adventure for me, because my brother was so different now—almost like my father, except that he lived in a furnished room, not in a house full of people. He wanted to know about the raft, so I told him I'd sailed it and had put it away for the winter.

"You come down next summer and we'll sail it together, the way we'd planned," I said.

"No," he said. "We've *already* sailed it together. It's all yours now."

My own son is sixteen years old now, and has made me aware lately that his mother and I have been quarreling for some time. Nothing new, of course—the same general quarrel—but neither his mother nor I had ever before noticed that it annoyed him. Later on this year, or perhaps next year, I know he's going to have a talk with *his* younger brother, and then take off. I want to be ready when that happens, so I can keep his mother from trying to stop him. He's a good boy, and I don't mind at all that he thinks I've made a mess of my life, which is one thing he is *not* going to do.

Of course he isn't.

THE DUEL

TRASH BASHMANIAN WAS VERY GOOD at public speaking, although he was better at pitching horseshoes and dueling. He was also quite good at taking a dare, and would jump off a high branch of a tree as if it were nothing. The dueling was real swordsmanship, which was taught him by a Frenchman who lived on L Street, not from our house in Fresno, and who somehow persuaded somebody to let him give free lessons to kids at the nearby California Playground every afternoon from four to five and all day Saturday.

The announcement appeared one day on the bulletin board at the playground, and Trash and several of his Portuguese pals and Armenian cousins, seeing the word "free" in the notice, were there the following afternoon for the first lesson. "I've been dueling all my life," Trash said to the Frenchman, referring to the stick duels he had enjoyed with anybody at school who had been willing to take him on. But the Frenchman produced a pair of ancient foils, authentic dueling devices surely brought over from his lost life in Paris, and was able to demonstrate that dueling wasn't quite just a matter of thrashing about with broomsticks. It was a courteous if deadly sport, very near the outskirts of art. Trash soon became his star pupil, and Trash's favorite expression became "On guard!"

Trash, older than me by two or three years, was a real friend as well as a first cousin, and he was excessively cheerful for a Bashmanian. For instance, he never thought of his first name as an insult or even a friendly disparagement, no matter who said it. "Trash" was actually only an ignorant American rendering of his perfectly proper Armenian name, Artarash. The first teacher he had had at Emerson School hadn't been able to pronounce the name, so Artarash became Trash, and by the time Trash was eight or nine he had almost forgotten Artarash. He was twelve going on thirteen when he took up dueling, and was already a champion horseshoe thrower. He was certainly always able to throw a ringer at will, especially for a penny bet. As for taking a dare, he stood alone in our whole world, until one day, after highdiving into the very shallow water of Thompson Ditch, near Malaga, and almost breaking both arms, he suddenly realized that for years he had been risking his life for no profit whatever. A few days later, he remarked, as if he had gone into another line of business, "I don't take dares anymore," and that was the end of the matter.

At this time, back in 1919, public speaking was a highly regarded talent in Fresno, and Trash was the best talker in town. He did his speaking at schools, churches, picnics, and Fourth of July celebrations. In a pinch, he could be counted on to use up anywhere from five to twenty-five minutes, without preparation. He spoke in a voice that was not his regular voice. It had a higher pitch, and as it went along it acquired a rather musical quality, almost as if he were humming the speech or even singing it, and now and then during his speeches he actually broke into songs, to illustrate something or other that he thought needed illustrating.

Trash could talk on any subject, most likely because he

knew that nobody was really listening in any case. During a talk at the Courthouse Park, for instance, he suddenly said, "That is why we have the Fourth of July," even though the preceding part of the speech had been about the Conestoga wagon. What's more, he heard instant applause. In the tradition of popular oratory, Trash started a talk at random, moved confidently ahead in no particular direction, and, although he spoke very clearly, said nothing.

After Masoor Franswah (as his students were instructed to call him) had taught him dueling, Trash frequently during a speech made a classical charge followed by a withdrawal movement, without explanation. He also kicked his right leg backward three or four times, again without explanation. Once when he did this, during a speech on civic pride, at the Parlor Lecture Club, his audience of women, eager to be cultured, burst into joyous giggles, accompanied by applause, which Trash believed was for what he had just said.

"What was that backward kicking for?" I asked him on our way home.

"I had a cramp. I had to kick it out," Trash said.

"What about the dueling?"

"What dueling?"

"Three or four times during your talk, you did some dueling."

"How did it go over?" he asked.

"All right, I guess," I said. "But what was it for?"

"Just a little decoration."

"But you've done the backward kicking and the dueling in the last three public speeches you've made."

"I get a cramp, I kick backwards. I need a decoration, I make a decoration," Trash said.

"I thought you were practicing, so you could duel some-body," I said. "I mean the way they used to duel in the old days—for keeps. At dawn, down by the river, for honor."

"Yes, that is what I want to do," Trash said.

"With real swords?"

"Yes, with real swords."

"For keeps?"

"I'll decide that at the time of the duel," Trash said. "I'll draw blood, but I may not kill."

"When's it going to be?"

"According to Masoor Franswah, two things are neces-sary," Trash said. "I've got to be insulted. Then I hit him on both sides of the face with a glove, and he's got to accept the challenge."

"Have you got a glove?"

"I've got the glove I wear when I play left field."

"You hit him across the face with *that* and he'll accept the challenge, all right," I said.

"I hope so," Trash said.

"Who's it going to be?" I asked.

"Who's been insulting me?"

"How about Miss Clifford?" I said. This was his teacher at Emerson School.

"Miss Clifford insults everybody in the sixth grade," Trash said. "Besides, it's got to be a man."

"A boy, don't you mean?"

"A boy's insults don't count," Trash said. "You hit him one in the nose and that's the end of it. If I'm going to swipe— if I'm going to borrow Masoor Franswah's swords and draw blood and maybe kill, it's got to be a man. So who's been pass-ing remarks behind my back? In the male adult community?"

"Nobody, Trash," I said. "Everybody likes you. You make these patriotic public speeches. You start them all just right and end them all just right. 'Mr. Chairman, Mrs. Chairman, Mrs. Chairman's mother, Dr. Rowell, Mr. Setrakinn, members of the Board of Education, ladies and gentlemen, boys and girls,' and all that other stuff at the beginning. And then at the end, how about the prayer that you say, that makes tears come to the eyes of so many people? 'Almighty God, let me try to be like Lincoln, not like Booth.' Who's Booth, Trash?"

"The dirty little sneak that shot Mr. Lincoln, that's who," Trash said. "Listen, has anybody been passing remarks behind your back? You're my kid cousin, you know."

"I don't think so, excepting members of the family," I said, "but it's always in front of my back."

"Members of the family don't count, either," Trash said. "Think hard. Who do I hate?"

"You don't hate anybody, Trash. Unless it's that dirty little sneak, Booth."

"He's been dead for years," Trash said. "I know I hate somebody, but I just can't seem to remember who. Let me think. Isn't there somebody we all hate?"

"Each other once in a while, is all I can remember."

"That's different."

"How about Masoor Franswah?"

"He's my friend," Trash said. "That little Frenchman taught me everything I know about being civilized."

"Do you hate Italians, maybe?" I asked.

"No, of course not."

"How about Germans? Indians? Mexicans? Hindus? Japanese? Serbians? Chinese? Portuguese? Negroes? Spaniards?"

"No, I like them all."

"Then you better forget about drawing blood," I said.

"It isn't a matter of forgetting," Trash said. "It's a matter of honor."

"What *is* honor?" I said. "I mean, what is it?"

"Honor?"

"Yes, Trash."

"Well, honor is . . . *yourself*. Every Bashmanian in the world has got a lot of himself."

"I never heard of any of them dueling anybody," I said.

"I'm the first Bashmanian who knows how. Find out who I hate and let me know, will you?"

The next day, he came to my house, and I was ready for him. "Trash," I said, "I think I found out who you hate."

"Who?"

"Turks."

"You're right," he said. "I *knew* there was somebody I hate. Now we're getting somewhere." He picked up a stick and began to duel, and he looked very good. "Who's a Turk, in town?"

"We've got Assyrians, Syrians, Persians, and maybe a few Arabs," I said.

"There's got to be a Turk somewhere in town, too," Trash said.

"Well, there's Ahboudt," I said. "You know—the man I work for in the Free Market Saturdays. I'm there from six in the morning until three in the afternoon, for twenty-five cents and a paper sack full of whatever he's stuck with. How about *him*?"

"Ahboudt? *Sounds* Turkish," Trash said. "Ask him. Let me know."

The following Saturday, I asked Ahboudt, and he looked at me in a funny way, and then he said, "Shine the eggplants, please." At the end of the day, when he gave me the quarter, he said, "Are you asking the Turk question for the government, or for yourself?"

"For myself, Mr. Ahboudt."

"I am not a Turk," he said. "I am an Arab." And then, "Christian."

"Do you know a Turk?" I asked.

"Why?"

"My cousin Trash wants to duel him."

"Why does he want to do that?"

"Trash likes everybody except Turks," I said, "and you only duel people you don't like. Is there a Turk somewhere in town?"

"There was a Turk," Ahboudt said, "but he was an old man and he died."

I passed along this information to Trash, who said, "I've got to find me a Turk. Enough is enough. I've got an idea. Be ready at seven o'clock at your house, and I'll take you with me to the Civic Auditorium tonight."

"The wrassling matches?"

"No, they're having New Citizens' Night. Maybe one of them will be a Turk, God willing."

"Are you going to make a public speech?"

"I may be called on to address the new Americans," Trash said.

When he came by at a quarter to seven and we started

walking to the Civic Auditorium, I said, "Have you got your speech ready?"

"I think so."

"What's your topic this time?"

"If Mayor Toomey asks me to get up on the stage and talk for ten minutes, the way he usually does, I'm going to say something about the real meaning of America."

"What are you going to say?"

"In America we forget old hatreds," Trash said. "Now nobody is anybody else's enemy. We are all members of the same family. We are all Americans. When we arrived in America, we stopped being what we were for so long."

I recognized this as something I had already heard six or seven times in class at Emerson School.

"Well, I don't think the Bashmanians stopped being what *they* were," I said.

Trash brought his outfielder's glove from the back pocket of his pants and studied it, and then he studied me.

"What's the matter?" I said.

"You're the first man who has ever insulted me," he said. "Me, Trash Bashmanian, patriotic American. And you're my own kid cousin, my own *first* kid cousin. I've known you all your life. I don't know what to do."

"Well, don't hit me with that glove," I said, "because I don't know anything about dueling, and if I insulted you I didn't mean to, and I apologize."

"Thank God," Trash said. "Apology accepted. Don't ever do it again—you don't know what happened to me when you said what you said."

"What happened?"

"My blood boiled."

"I'm sorry," I said, "but I was really surprised when you said that in America nobody is anybody else's enemy, because for two weeks I've been looking all over town for a Turk for you to duel and maybe kill."

"So what?" Trash said. "When you find the Turk, let me know, that's all. I'll think of something."

At the Civic Auditorium, we took seats in the first row, and right from the beginning everything began to go a little wrong, which was all right with me. At ten minutes to eight, Mayor Toomey said, "Dr. Chester Rowell, who is to make the main talk of the evening has been unavoidably detained, and Miss Shakay Takmakjian, who is to render a violin solo, has not yet arrived, so our program is unfortunately off schedule. We have a few minutes of spare time, and therefore it gives me great pleasure to call on our young friend Trash Bashmanian to come up here and . . . say something."

Trash jumped out of his seat, ran to the steps, and was standing beside Mayor Toomey by the time the Mayor said, "Ladies and gentlemen, Trash Bashmanian."

Crossing himself quickly but almost casually, like a professional man of God, Trash launched into another of his famous public addresses.

"What is America?" he asked in his high-pitched, special voice, and that was all he needed to get the glory and the oratory rolling. Soon he was asking a lot of other unanswerable questions, and talking smoothly, and now and then suddenly dueling or kicking backward. After about twelve minutes, it seemed as if Trash was about to bring his talk to an end, but Mayor Toomey called out from the side of the stage, "A few minutes more, Trash," and Trash changed from a concluding tone to a tone of starting up again. He was just getting into the swing of this new start when Mayor Toomey called out, "Tie it up, Trash. Here he is." And so, simultaneously dueling and kicking backward, Trash paused, looked upward, and said, "Almighty God, let me try to be like Woodrow Wilson, not Henry Ford."

The audience rose to its feet and broke into applause— perhaps because the first citizen of the city, Dr. Chester Rowell, had just appeared on the stage. Trash bowed, but only once, and came down the steps and sat down.

On our way home, I said, "You sure told 'em, Trash."

"What did I say?"

"You said we are all brothers—all of us—just as Washington, Jefferson, Jackson, and Caruso taught us to be."

"Who?"

"That's what I was wondering."

"Did I put Caruso in there with those other guys?" he asked.

"Yes. What'd you do it for?"

"I don't know," Trash said, "but there must be a reason."

"And then you sang 'O Sole Mio,' " I said.

"I knew there was a reason," Trash said. "It was so I could sing the song he sings on that Victor Red Seal phonograph record at our house. How was my voice?"

"It was good," I said.

"Was my diction all right, singing the Italian words?"

"I guess so," I said. "It certainly sounded like Italian to me. You won't be wanting me to find a Turk any more then, will you?"

"Why not?"

"Because you told me in your speech not to."

"I *did?*" Trash said.

"Yes. Don't you remember when you were coming to the end of the talk the first time—before Mayor Toomey told you to keep going? Well, you were almost singing a lot of other things, kind of humming the words, and then all of a sudden you said, 'Look not in the world for the Turk, you will not find him there.'"

"'Look not in the world for the Turk, you will not find him there'?" Trash repeated.

"That's right."

We walked along in silence for quite a while, and then Trash said, "Was it a good public speech, would you say?"

"Very good," I said.

"As good as my others?"

"Better," I said. "But no more of this Turk business then—is that right? No duel, no drawing of blood? 'Look not in the world for the Turk, you will not find him there.' That's what you said, Trash."

"What a fool I was," Trash said. "Now what am I going to do with all this dueling talent?"

What he did was have me take lessons from Masoor Franswah, so that now and then we could take turns being the Turk in the world, and in our own hearts, each of us winning and losing every time, whichever side we took.